AUTUMN RAIN

A
Love Story

By
A A Pratt

AUTUMN RAIN

ISBN # 978-1-7345872-7-2

iii

This book is dedicated to the memory of
Kealoha.

AUTUMN RAIN

FORWARD

The setting is much like you would have found near the Pacific Coast of Northern California in the mid 1950's. This was a period after the close of the Second World War when the middle class was beginning to acquire some social and economic upward mobility. Eisenhower was President. Some who had worked in the war plants had put aside enough money to buy a couple of acres of land and begin settling down to a better life than the one left behind in Oklahoma, Texas, Arkansas, or wherever they came from. The newcomers were given names by the locals such as "Okies," "Texans," "Arkies" or whatever name could be made up, indicating a lower class of interloper and definitely not a native. The newcomers had already suffered many indignities by the 50's and quietly accepted the name calling as a part of the initiation fee to a better life. Eventually most of them were assimilated and became part of the local culture. Minorities were somewhat more visible, and their acceptance was slow to be realized. There were only a few Blacks, some Asians, and some Hispanics in this area. Their names had more of social bite to them, "Spooks," "Gooks" and "Spiks," were common. Servicemen were returning from overseas with war brides from around the world. The offspring of those unions did not always find it easy going. For people who were Japanese and lived here during the war it was even harder. They spent the war years in guarded internment camps. This was the background of the mid-fifties in which this story takes place.

A.   A.   PRATT

AUTUMN RAIN

Contents

AUTUMN RAIN

AUTUMN RAIN

xi

AUTUMN RAIN

AUTUMN RAIN

CHAPTER 1

THE LAST RIDE

It was raining. It had rained for a month it seemed. It was not really raining hard—just drizzling and making things wet and useless and depressing. The windshield wipers were beating out a rhythm to the slow methodical drizzle.

I came to the familiar white fence and turned into the long driveway. I looked at the house at the end. It was a large sprawling single-story structure with a large plate glass window facing the road.

The huge pine tree to the side seemed to convey in some unexplained way that this was the country. I could not picture a tree like that in town, although I suppose there were some. I had been here countless times these last three months, but today the house seemed different, not warm and inviting. Now it seemed dreary. Maybe it was just the rain making it seem that way, or maybe it was gray sky and the white paint. I do not know exactly what made it seem cold and bare, but it certainly suited the mood I was in. I looked in the big window as I approached the house. I could see you standing inside with your coat on. Your bags were on the floor beside you. You looked out and saw me. I left the motor running. As I stepped from the car into the drizzle, I buckled my raincoat and pulled the collar up to keep the rain from my neck.

I watched you emerge from the front door, placing the luggage on the step one bag at a time, making three trips in all. I walked slowly through the rain toward you. You smiled. I could feel the tenseness under the smile. I smiled back barely masking my own tension. One might have assumed we were total strangers about to take a ride in the rain. We both knew that was not the case. By some unspoken agreement we adopted a pleasant air of cordiality. I wondered if we could maintain this facade all fifty miles to the train station.

"Is that everything?" I asked flatly.

"Yes," you answered in a similar tone.

I put the bags in the car, opened the door for you and waited until you pulled in your long white coat so it would not get caught in the door. I walked slowly, deliberately, around the car and climbed in. I did not turn the car around but backed it down the driveway to the road. I had to lean out of the door because the rear window was fogged from the weather. At the end of the driveway, I turned the car and started down the road.

"Want to listen to the radio?" I asked politely.

"I'll get it," you said reaching for the knob. You were no stranger in this car, and you had played that radio many times in the last three months.

I took the opportunity of looking at you while your attention was on the radio. You had not changed, I thought. You were still beautiful. The prettiest girl I had ever seen and the prettiest I would ever know. Your black hair and Asiatic eyes and the soft, less-than-olive, color of your skin were as lovely as I had always thought. Your slender, well-proportioned body was obvious even through your dress and that bulky coat. For a young woman of twenty-one years, you seemed quite mature. You seemed as if you knew what you wanted and knew how to get it. I wondered if you were right. I had some doubts.

Just then you finished with the radio and sat back in the seat. I shifted my gaze for fear you would see me out of the corner of your eye.

"What time do you have to catch the train?" I tried to sound impersonal.

"Three-thirty." You looked straight ahead at the road.

I looked at my watch. It was just two o'clock. We had an hour and a half to get to the station. I could make it easily if the rain did not get too bad. The train station. You were really going. I had hoped you would not. I had done everything I could think of to keep you from going, but there seemed to be no way to prevent you. Well, what's done is done. A short ride of fifty odd miles and you would be gone. Gone. Three months together ending in a car ride. Funny, it began with a car ride and it was ending with a car ride. At least that was consistent. I thought of all the car rides we had taken.

CHAPTER 2

THE FIRST RIDE

It was Autumn, almost three months ago, before the rains came

"Do you have any classes this afternoon?" I asked.

"One," You answered.

"When?"

"Two to three. Why?"

"Well, I have to drive over to the hospital this afternoon. I thought perhaps you might like to ride over. I drive the road every day and I do not like to ride the whole twenty miles alone if I can help it.

Besides, it is such a beautiful day that it shouldn't be wasted."

"I'll have to call mother and tell her not to pick me up. When do you want to leave?"

"As soon as you are through at three. I will meet you after class. OK?"

"OK."

I was not sure why I had asked you to go. I really did not expect you to accept my invitation. You had always turned down every other offer I had made that involved our being alone. You seemed to like it when I came to your house to visit but never wanted to go out. Ah, but this was different. You wanted to go this time. What a beautiful day!

"Hi," you said with eagerness, a bit subdued, but with eagerness, nonetheless.

"Well, it's three and you're free so let's go," I bubbled.

You sat there across the car from me, very relaxed, sitting side-saddle in the seat and slid off your shoes. Rolling down the window you adjusted the wind wing.

"Mm... It's hot and the breeze feels good."

"Yes, it does. Doesn't it?" I echoed.

"You drive this road every day to work?"

"Uh huh. Well, not every day. Sometimes I go over the mountain. That one off to the right there. It's a short-cut. 'Course the road's a bit kinky, but the scenery is nice."

Neither of us spoke much on the way over. I deliberately delayed coming back so that we could take the return trip over the mountain as the sun went down. I timed it perfectly. We reached the crest of the climb and looked out into the western sky before us. The sun seemed reluctant to leave and crept slowly away leaving patches of soft colors hanging from every bush and tree as though to mark the way for a return trip tomorrow.

It was Autumn. Autumn that held such majesty for me. I have often tried to analyze the tremendous emotional impact of Autumn but have never quite succeeded. Perhaps it is the colors. The light, gay, golden leaves; the delicate browns, a bit sad and pleasant at once; the permanent crisp greens; the soft gentle wind that lifts and moves and bathes things making it all a world of fantasy. The sifting, rolling, dipping, breathing air softened everything into a reality of dreams. All capped by the changing blue and shot through with feathery shafts of a flickering spectrum.

We felt such things as could not be expressed in words, for words are not so endowed. Words are too crude, to noisy, too real for this half unreal sensation. And so, it was we did not speak but just breathed in the air and memories with it. I knew when I left you at your door that I would see you again... soon.

CHAPTER 3

THE FIRST KISS

The very next evening I called to see if you would like to go for a ride with me to return a book to a friend. You said you would like very much to go. I picked you up at your door ten minutes later.

"Hi," you said climbing into the car.

"Hi."

"Will we be gone long?"

"Not too long. I have to go to work tonight so I'll have to be home and get ready for work by nine-thirty."

"Let's see...It's only six-thirty now. OK. Let's go."

I drove to the other side of town and delivered the book. The book was overdue but there was still no hurry to return it. It was just an excuse to be alone with you again.

"Would you like some coffee?" I asked trying to extend our time.

"Yes. I would," you answered.

From the very first moment I wanted to pull you to me and kiss you, but I was afraid you would resist any such attempt. We finished the coffee, and it was only a little after seven o'clock. I could not think of any further reason to detain us, so I said I guessed we had better get home. You agreed and we left. You lived with your folks five miles out of town in the country. On the way I was suddenly struck with the uncontrollable desire to kiss you. I stopped the car along the road where no one passed often, and we could be comparatively alone. I monkeyed with the radio for a bit, avoiding your gaze, because I did not know what to say if you asked what I was doing and why we stopped. I was sure you knew, but I was not really sure at all. I knew I was going to kiss you, but I did not know just how to begin. I started a thousand times to reach for your hand, but each time did not go through with it. I felt the same way as the time I first tried to dive off a diving board. I remember standing there hesitating for what seemed like hours before I finally half-jumped, half-fell into the pool. I wanted to be a bit more in control of the situation this time. I knew I was going to do it. I might as well get on with it. I calmly reached for your hand. I should not say calmly, because my heart was pounding something fierce. I even shut my eyes as if that would make rejection easier if it came. I touched your hand at last. Your hand was warm and responsive. You gripped my hand with the warmth and feeling I had only dared to hope for. My heart seemed to stop; I could not hear it anymore. I pulled you to me. Your handbag was in the way and I tossed it to the back seat and kissed you. How long I had dreamed of this moment. I wanted it to never end.

"I have wanted to do that for so long," I whispered.

"I have wanted you to do it for ever so long."

The moon was bright, and I could see your eyes earnestly searching my face as if looking for something. It was an almost adoring look. I have never been the object of such a look and suddenly felt strong and invincible. I felt giddy as I pulled you close and kissed you with an almost frenzied gentleness. I held you, not wanting to ever let go, as if you had imbued me with a power that would fade if I ever let go. I held you for what seemed a mental eternity and only let go when I felt sure you would not disappear.

Finally, your lips moved and my whole being tingled with the sound of your voice. Your resonant breath said something about wanting to spend the whole night here with me. Your body was vibrant and warm, and I yearned. I knew I had to leave shortly for work and that enhanced, rather than diminished, the statement. Just your saying it was enough for now.

I checked my watch. It was later than I thought.

"We'll have to leave now."
I left you at your door and was at work before I knew it.

The whole thing: having you alone, kissing you, talking to you and hearing you express some warmth toward me, it had taken so long that it didn't seem possible it could be happening. After all those years of adoration from afar and now this magical reunion, it had to be destiny at work.

CHAPTER 4

"I'M NO GOOD"

T he weekend came and we found ourselves parked in the moonlight. "You comfortable?" I asked. You moved your shoulders in an indescribable way that women do and said, "Uh huh."

I was looking into your eyes, your beautiful eyes. You were smiling with your eyes half shut. The clouded moon was dim, and you could not see my eyes. I do not know why you wanted to see my eyes. I suppose there must have been a reason though because you did not seem be at ease until you could. We laid there just looking at each other for some time, not talking, just feeling, feeling needed and loved. We were removed from the world around, linked only by the radio and its soft music, just laid there warm and full inside. I moved my hand to touch your cheek. The mere touch initiated a series of impulses that welled and surged into a driving sea of desire, blindly, surely finding your lips, and ebbing into a calm sea of tranquility only after some time.

"You happy?" I asked.

"Mm, very," you whispered.

"I love you," I said.

"You shouldn't."

"Why?"

"Because I'm no good."

"What do you mean?"

"Just that. I'm no good."

"That's silly. I do not care about the past. I love you here and now and that's all that matters," I said dismissively.

We kissed and were silent with our own private thoughts for some time. My musings carried me off into a world where I saw you as my wife. I was trying to picture how it might be. Could I make you happy? Would you grow tired of me? It scared me to think you might. I wanted to tell you that we should get married to preserve our love for each other, but how could I ask you to marry me when I did not know where I was going. I could not make up my mind as to what I wanted to do. I only knew I wanted to be creative and follow a star I had yet to find. "Stupid," I thought. "you are getting way ahead of yourself. I know she feels something for me. Tomorrow is another day."

"Can you drive me to a service station?"

"Sure."

The following night at work I had some spare time. I wanted to talk to you, but, of course, you were not there, and I could not so the next best thing was to write you a letter. Since I would not see you except when we were at school, I decided I would mail you this letter to be sure I did not forget to tell you everything I wanted to say. When we had lunch together, we did not always remember to talk about important things, so it would be better to write you a letter while thoughts were fresh in my head. I would rather say these things in person, but with you dancing with your sister during the evenings in the city fifty miles away and me working all night and going to school in the afternoon, we had little time together to talk. I picked up a pencil and wrote:

"Dear Princess,

"There are those who say love begets love. It may be so; I do not know. I hope it is so."

I could not find the words to continue, to properly express my concerns, and I just tore up the unfinished letter and threw it in the trash. I would have to do it face to face when the time was right.

CHAPTER 5

CORN STALKS

The ground was still wet from the night's rain, and the sunlight which is the source and carrier of daylight colors, was displaying more of its spectrum as it glittered through the little bubbles of water that covered everything in view. I sat in the car in front of the campus library waiting. The noon bell rang, and you were sitting beside me. We had coffee and we drove away to a nearby secluded road on the outskirts of town. We had hardly spoken the whole time, but words seemed small compared to our physical presence.

"Boo!" I said attempting playful affection.

"Boo."

"I missed you," I said as you moved closer.

"Why?"

"Why??? How should I know? Some things can't be explained."

You did not respond, just sat there. I did not expect you to say anything. It occurred to me then that you seldom said very much. I always felt I knew what you were thinking, and words seemed sometimes redundant. You were doing that now. Looking at me, then away fleetingly, all the while pursing, half biting your ever so slightly quivering lips. The total impression I felt was that you were experiencing some pleasant emotion which was about to express itself. Your eyes with their fascinating natural lift at the corners added to the whole look a kind of languid, fawn-like innocence. The look transpired so quickly as to be almost imperceptible in time, but the effect was as though you had spoken a book.

I did the only appropriate thing possible. I kissed you. Your head was on my shoulder. I looked past you to the cornfield that composed my entire view. The ragged stalks still stood, turning brown in the November sun. Although they typified an erect graveyard, they also had a kind of beauty about them. To the average person here was a useless field of decaying life, the last stage before the burial. But how much more it seemed now. They seemed proud standing there, resigned that they had done what they had to do. They had given of themselves what was ordained, suffered the bearing of their fruit, and now there was nothing left for them to do but retire to the earth from where they came for a long winter's rest.

CHAPTER 6

BACKGROUND

"I can't hear you," you were saying.

"Well, I don't wonder, everyone is talking too loud and the television is blaring. Hold on, I'll turn it down."

I picked up the phone again and this time you could hear me.

"How was school today?" I asked.

"Fine," she said. "Oh, I need a book. Do you have Virgil's Aeneid?"

"Sure. When do you want it?"

"Oh, in the next two or three minutes."

"I'll bring it over tomorrow. That be soon enough?"

"What time tomorrow?"

"Let's see...you have to work tonight so you'll want to sleep late. I have to work tonight, and I'll sleep late so how about sometime tomorrow afternoon?"

"Call before you come to be sure I'm up."

"Fine. Oh, by the way, Pop asked me to ask you if you would dine out with us."

"When?" she asked.

"Well, you're off next Monday. So how about Monday night?"

"I don't care. How about you?"

"Alright with me. I want you to meet Mother and she is anxious to meet you."

"OK. Monday it is. Look, I'm sorry but I've got to get ready for work now."

"I'll see you tomorrow then," I said.

"OK. 'Bye...." (click). I hung up and felt good. As I passed pop's chair to turn up the television he asked in an interested voice:

"Was that my girl?"

"Yes, only she's my girl, not yours."

"She going to dinner with us?"

"Next Monday evening."

(Television) *"When you're having friends in -*

At a party or to dine-

Take home a bottle of Roma- America's favorite wine- And now back to the adventures of......"

"Turn it down!" Mother shouted.

I reduced the volume and sat waiting for dinner.

I thought I would watch television, but my eyes lighted on the portrait I had just finished. It seemed more interesting than the adventures of whoever the adventures were of and I studied it. I enjoyed painting it although it was not the girl in this portrait, but her sister that I had fallen in love with. Perhaps I liked it because there was a strong resemblance, the same lift at the corners of the eyes, the same black hair, the same delicate skin tones. Those tones were a real challenge, a dash of alizarin, a touch of cadmium yellow, a small bit of burnt umber and lots of zinc white. Then the lightest touch of green and blue around the eyes. Yes, I liked the picture. It was true that it lacked a certain intangible spark that I had managed to somehow create in your portrait, but no one mentioned the difference. The pictures were well matched I thought. I would deliver this one tomorrow. Your mother would be pleased. I could use the $75.00.

I remember painting the first portrait, the one of you. I worked on it day and night for a week. I remember it seemed unfair to charge for it. It had been so much fun I really did not want to part with it. Not even for $75.00. But a deal is a deal.

That picture probably started the whole romance. I suppose I should say, rather, that it set it in motion for it had started long before that in Junior High School when I saw you for the first time. That must have been seven years ago. It did not seem that long ago. Your black hair and dark eyes with your lithe, slender frame were the embodiment of a boyish dream of mine. You were a perfect little island Princess. The kind you dream of meeting on some tropic isle. That exotic image of you remained in my mind these past seven years.

I only ever saw you at a distance until I was in High School. I worked a paper route and was enthralled to learn that you lived on my route and your parents took the paper. Even then we seldom saw each other and even less often spoke. I was very bashful and self-conscious. I lived with my folks in a shack. When we moved here from the city, it was just a bare plot of two acres, and we lived several years in a surplus army squad tent sixteen feet by thirty-two feet on bare ground for a floor. Pop was a good carpenter and we slowly built the shack from the ground up. First a floor, then walls up to five feet underneath the tent, keeping the tent for a roof for two years more until the seams of the canvas began to rot. Then one night a heavy rain and wind ripped the tent over my bed, and I got soaked. The roof came that spring. In the meantime, I learned how to stitch canvas in the rain. The shack we now lived in was a big upgrade in comfort and self-esteem. We had some windows and a regular door and even running water from a dug well and pump. Both of my folks worked and getting ahead was still slow, but there would eventually be a real house like everyone else. Pop always finished what he started, and I learned many skills as his helper. Living as we did was a sensitive point for me when I had to wait out front for the school bus. I was embarrassed, but never let on. You, on the other hand, lived in a big sprawling white house with huge plate-glass windows with beautiful curtains. There was a long white picket fence from the house to the road and a big, lush lawn. I could not help feeling a bit inadequate.

During the summers you and your sister went away dancing from here to New York at hotels and resorts. You and your sister were even extras in a movie in Hollywood. After high school you were gone, and I went off to college in Utah for a year. When I came home, I did not see you for over a year. Perhaps I would never have seen you again if it had not been for that strange incident. One evening, not too long ago, I was driving into town when, for no reason at all, it occurred to me to stop and say hello to your folks. I do not know what gave me the notion at the time. It was even more strange that when I arrived your mother told me you had just called from Chicago, and during the conversation, you asked if they had seen me and how was I. During that visit I saw the photo you had sent home. It prompted me to ask if I could borrow it to paint a portrait.

The portrait stirred me to write you a letter. It seemed to me odd that I had never thought of writing a letter before. It was ridiculous. I supposed I had not written because I felt it would be useless and I would embarrass myself. I was sure you had no feelings for me. Now everything was different. The second letter was better than the first draft, which I tore up. I poured out my soul. I did not expect a reply, and none came. At least I had expressed my secret feelings and that made me feel better.

Then that day a month ago...no three months ago, when I was registering at junior college, I heard a familiar voice and turned to see your sister standing there smiling. I could not speak for my gaping mouth. I knew you had come home. The first time I....

"Hey, do you want to eat dinner or not?" Mother interrupted my reminiscing.

"Yes, Mom, be right there."

CHAPTER 7

A LOOK OF FEAR

With a book in one hand and the portrait of your sister in the other I knocked on the door. I could see you through the window sitting in the living room in a white robe and a hairnet. You had obviously slept late for it was now 5:30 PM. Your sister answered the door and you scampered frantically out of sight.

"Come in and sit down," your sister invited. "She'll be out in a minute."

I placed Virgil's Aeneid on the mantle then hung the painting on the right side of the fireplace opposite the matching portrait on the left. I had already driven the nail, so I just hung the picture and stepped back to see if it was hanging straight. The whole family came to see the portraits. They all were standing in front of me and I was suddenly aware you were behind me. I reached back without looking and pulled you to me, then turned to investigate your smiling face.

"Hi, sleepy head," I grinned.

"Hi."

"How long have you slept?"

"Fourteen hours."

"Well, that should hold you for a while."

"Uh huh. Oh. Did you bring the book?"

"It's on the mantel."

By this time, the family had disbanded. I noticed they were pleased. You asked me to sit down and went to get some coffee. I watched you move gracefully, swiftly to the kitchen and disappear. You artfully concealed your embarrassment about being seen so soon after waking and not quite ready to be looked at. You could not know that in my eyes you could only look beautiful regardless the circumstances. I have observed that un-made-up people are often more genuine and unpretentious to be with.

"Here's your coffee."

"Thanks," I said, making room beside me. I looked into your eyes and felt a warm glow. The look on your face was peaceful and pleasant. You went to get your coffee and I leaned back, lit a cigarette, and closed my eyes.

I heard the cup clink on the coffee table. You were looking at me when I opened my eyes. For a split second I thought I saw a great fear in your face. It startled me. I had not seen that there before. Although I kind of suspected it might be there, I had not seen it until now. My mind dwelt on it. What could it be you were so afraid of? It was not me. But what then? I yearned to be alone with you to find out. I knew....

"Hey, stop dreaming," you were saying.

"I'm sorry." I looked at my watch. "Gee, It's late. I've got to go."

"When will I see you again?"

"Tomorrow is Sunday and I'm going to sleep all day. I work tonight, but I go to school Monday, so I'll see you Monday evening."

CHAPTER 8

WHAT TO DO

Monday evening was dark, no moon. The rain hammered an unceasing staccato rhythm on the roof of the car. The radio was playing soft music that blended with the noise of the rain. The whole effect was soft and pleasant. I had leveled the back of the seat into a flat surface - a nice feature of this car. Just move a lever and you were lying flat. We laid there side by side looking out into the rainy night.

"I like the rain," you were saying.

"So do I."

"How do you feel about changing your mind?" you asked abruptly.

"What do you mean?"

"Do you remember when, not too long ago, you said you wanted to be a doctor?"

"Yes, I remember," I said.

"Well, now you say you don't want to be a doctor. How do you feel about changing your mind?"

"Oh, do you mean...a... I still don't know what you mean."

"I guess I just can't say it any other way. I just mean _how_ do you feel about it?"

"Foolish and wise," I answered beginning to understand.

"Now what do _you_ mean?"

"Well, I change my mind so often that I feel foolish, but when it is obvious that I am wrong, and I change my mind then I feel wise."

"That was what I wanted to know."

"Well. Now that that is settled, why did you want to know?"

"I wanted to know if it was wrong to change your mind. I mean, well, I know it's supposed to be right and good to change your mind, but why shouldn't people always feel that way when they change their mind?"

"You mean if a person seems to be forever changing his mind, but still he doesn't seem to...?"

"No. I don't think you understand again," you said. "I mean it's fine to change your mind I guess, but don't other people think you're sort of unstable if you do it all the time?"

"Maybe they do," I said. "I know I feel pretty guilty about telling people I'm going to be a doctor one day and then telling them I want to be an artist the next. I begin to wonder about myself and what I am going to say the day after. I suppose people may think I'm unstable, but what else can I do?"

"I don't know. I wish I did. That is the way I feel too," you said.

"Do you think I'm unstable?" I asked.

"Not really, but I know you."

"You know, I have a hard time believing that most people are really sure what they want to do. You hear about people who knew what they wanted to do from the time they were kids. I have yet to meet one. The only thing I have been sure of is that I want to be the best at something or other, but I like everything. They say you should do what interests you. I am interested in everything. I sort of like the idea of being a doctor, but I love the idea of being an artist. I say I would like to be a doctor, and everyone is happy. When I suggest being an artist all I hear is "you cannot make a living at that, find something else."

"What are we supposed to do?" you puzzled.

"I wish I knew. From the time I was a little boy people always said I would be a great lawyer or something. I wish they had not said those things. It is frustrating to think I will never make it and disappoint them all. Why don't they tell us to just be what we believe in and not tell us what or how?"

"I don't know, but I agree," you sympathized.
I felt closer to you than before. Maybe we were two of a kind. I kissed you and time passed without seeming to.

"What do you want to do?" you continued.

"I plain don't know. I just don't know. I do know that I like to paint pictures, and write, and invent things and try to create something worthwhile. The person I most admire is Leonardo DaVinci. He did it all. I am no Leonardo, but he fascinates me. Everyone is eager to tell me what is important and worthwhile doing, but it is clear to me they do not know. I have to search this out for myself."

We did not resolve the question but felt closer for the discussion.

CHAPTER 9

"DON'T"

We had lunch and parked. Neither of us had a class until 2:00 PM and it was only 12:20 now. We did not speak for a while except to offer a cigarette back and forth. I could think of nothing important to say. I finally said, "I love you."

"Don't."

"Well, for Pete's sake why not?"

"You'll just get hurt."

"How? Why? What do you mean?"

You did not answer. Just got a "don't spoil it" look on your face. I was determined to pursue it. I felt this coming but had been afraid of what it would lead to. I thought it might die of neglect, but that did not happen. Now we would have to face it.

"Just what is it?" I asked.

"Let's don't."

"Look Princess, there's nothing we can't talk about. What is it?"

"Well, OK. It's Chicago...."

"So?"

"I'm going back."

"You sure that's what you want?" I asked trying not to sound wounded.

Eons of time passed, worlds of dreams were built, kingdoms and kings rose and fell into empty nothingness as you finally spoke.

"Ye-es."

I did not say anything. Everything had been said. I asked no questions, just looked at the sky and wondered if it might be a mirage that would suddenly be taken away. At last, I could only utter in what must have been a shaky voice,

"OK--if that's what you really want."

"Aren't you angry with me?"

"No. How could I? I think we both knew this might happen."

There was still nothing to say. I felt too hollow to pick up the pieces and try to put the dream back together. Some pieces were missing.

"Do you want to call it off right now?" I said hesitantly.

"Don't you think it would be better?"

"I asked you."

"Well, then I suppose so."

"I guess...I just can't understand it. Why? You can't tell me you don't love me. I won't believe it. I know better."

"You do?"

"Yes. At any rate there is no reason to stop just now. We have a dinner date with my folks tonight."

"You mean you still want me to go?"

"Of course. Nothing can change my mind about you. I still love you and that's that."

"But you wouldn't if you really knew me."

"Stop talking like that!"

"All right!"

"Fine!"

"I still don't see why you don't want to break it off now," you said.

"Probably for the same reason if I decided to quit smoking, I would do it gradually. Giving you up is going to be even harder."

We returned to school in time for class then went straight home. Mother had left for the store before I arrived, and I just sat there trying to reorganize my thoughts. I felt empty and betrayed. I prayed for the strength to do the right thing. After a time, I felt a bit better.

Mother returned from the store. We did not talk much. I tried to put on a pleasant face. Pop came home at 5:30 and we got ready to go out for dinner. They were eager to go. I was not sure I wanted to go.

CHAPTER 10

THE RESTAURANT

I picked you up at 6:30 PM. I was sullen but tried to smile. In the car it seemed incongruous that you moved close to me and gripped my arm. The sensation almost made me forget the day's unpleasantness.

The restaurant was cozy. Candlelight and music mellowed the atmosphere and produced a slight dreamlike quality that was relaxing. The room with its long, low ceiling was nearly empty but for us. The wallpaper was a deep, dull green background patterned with large pallid green leaves, dotted with small blossom-like pink-orange designs giving a soft vitality to the whole. The music seemed to come from the bar which was connected by a large square opening not unlike an archway. I introduced you and placed you between my parents and opposite myself. The conversation struggled at first but came freer with the food and wine.

"Do you suppose that is a candle inside that lamp or a light bulb?" I offered lightly.

"I think it's a light bulb," Pop said.

"I think so too," Mother chimed.

You did not offer an opinion. I decided to approach it scientifically by gathering all the available evidence, without looking. I placed my hand over the top opening. If it was a candle it should burn my hand. It did not, but it did seem hotter than a light bulb. I looked at the other tables to see if I could perceive some flickering. One was, but a man had just bumped that table and I could not be sure. Then I looked for an electrical cord. There were no wires visible. They could be buried. I decided it must be a candle, but then there seemed to be no way for it to get air. Now I was puzzled. It showed.

"Well, get up and look down the chimney," Mother said.

"I can't just get up and stand on a chair and look down the barrel of that thing," I protested.

"Well, you got me curious now. I'll do it myself," mother went on and actually did it.

I was a bit shocked. But it was cute the way she sat down and grinned: "It's a candle."

We ate the food and drank the wine and talked, and it was fun. It was obvious that my folks liked you. You were such a lady. A lovely lady at that.

CHAPTER 11

DREAMS

The dinner was over. I drove with you through the moonlit autumn countryside. We were in no hurry. It was early yet. I parked in a clearing off the road. Wined and dined and moonlight rich we sat, or rather, laid there at peace with all things.

"I like your parents. They're real people, nothing false or pretentious, simply good people."

"They like you."

"I'm so proud to have been with them."

"I'm glad. I was afraid you might not feel that way."

"Why?"

"I don't know. I guess I am always afraid people won't like things that belong to me. We have always been poor, and I get embarrassed because we don't live in a nice house and all."

"You shouldn't feel that way."

"I know."

"Mm. I had such a nice time," you sighed.

"So did I," I answered, kissing between words. Then kissing passionately with no words.
"Oh, I love you so...."

"Don't, please, don't."

"I don't understand how you can want me not to love you and say so, when we seem so good together."

"Well, it's because...I can't tell you."

"You must. I have to know!"

"Alright. You remember I told you I wanted money and security? I still do. I've tried not to, but it doesn't work."

"Just answer one question honestly. Will you do that?"

"Alright."

"Do you love me? Honestly?" I asked.

"Ye-y-es. I do."

"So, what is the problem?"

"I don't think you can give me the money and security that I need."

"There is more to this than that. The other night when I brought you a book, I saw a strange fear on your face. What were you afraid of? It can't be me."

"It's nothing."

"It can't be nothing. Please tell me."

"It's just a silly dream," you finally said. "You don't want to hear it. It sounds silly when you talk about it."

"I do want to hear it. Tell me."

"It's just a feeling I get."

"Tell me about it."

"It's a feeling that something or someone is coming to take away my mind or soul. It just gets closer and closer until I am screaming for God to take it away. Oh, it's too silly."

"No, it isn't."

"Well, it used to come...it has for almost two years...but didn't come as close. And now it comes in the form of friends and I don't recognize it until it's breathing on me. It's terrible! I just have to scream for God to take it away."

"What?"

"Didn't you hear what I said?"

"Yes, but what you just said...well, I'll be...if you hadn't said that just the way you did, I would never have consciously realized it."

"What are you talking about?"

"I can't ask you to believe it. It's too fantastic!"

"Tell me," you pleaded.

"It's just that I have had the same exact dream during the past two years! I know it sounds ridiculous, but so help me it's true."

"You're joking. This is no joking matter."

"If I describe the sound it makes would that convince you?"

"Maybe."

"Alright. This thing makes a humming noise. It makes you feel it is the devil coming to get your soul. The noise gets louder and louder until you wake up in a cold sweat telling God to take it away."

"You sure no one told you about my dream?"

"No one. Your sister told me you had bad dreams. Nothing more."

"It's unbelievable."
This weird dream sharing made us close and we felt a kinship from sharing it.

"What do you think it means?" you asked gravely serious.

"I don't know. I can only guess. Maybe we feel we do not deserve to be happy, that we feel guilty about something and the devil is coming to punish us. I do not really know. I just know we love each other, and we can't feel guilty about that."

"Maybe. I hope not."

The day had been full, from bad dreams to rejection and all points in between, finally reaching a pinnacle of pleasant peacefulness. The day, the dinner, the wine, the emotions were too much for both of us and we fell asleep.

CHAPTER 12

"I'M GOING TO CHICAGO"

I had not seen you for three days. It was dumb luck that it was not four days. I had no classes today, so I slept until 11:30 AM. When I got up it was raining. I timed getting dressed so I could just make it to pick you up at the library. Everything was fine until I tried to start the car. The battery was dead. I called the service station, but Rich was alone and could not leave to deliver a battery. He finally talked to a customer who was headed my way and agreed to drop off the new battery. I was only ten minutes late.

You got into the car and you looked at your clothes. There were rain spots all over them. The windows were fogged from the heater. The inside of the car was warm and a bit stuffy. Things seemed out of sorts and disjointed.

"Well, it's raining, and you like the rain," I said. "You should be happy with this day."

"I suppose so," you smiled back, not quite able to ignore the wet reality of your dress.

We had our customary cup of coffee and drove away to sit and talk.

"There's our cornfield," you said pointing out the window as I parked.

"Yes. You'd think all this rain would wash the mud from the stalks. It only seems to splash more mud on instead."

"That's true. It does. I think nature has her own rules."

We sat and looked at each other for a while. We did that a lot.

"I say, old girl, would it shock you if I said I missed you considerably?"

"Not in the least, old boy," you mimicked lightheartedly.

"Anything on your mind today?"

"Don't be silly. Of course not."

Absent a quick comeback, I kissed you and said, "I say, wasn't that a bit of alright?"

I did have something to say.

"I've made up my mind what I want to do."

"You mean for a living?"

"Yes."

"What did you decide?"

"I decided I like to help people. So many people are mixed up and confused, I want to help them be able to see that life is good. Since I lose sight of that myself, maybe it would help me too." You seemed only half impressed by this grand declaration. "You don't seem very enthusiastic about my decision."

"I have a feeling you are saying it for my benefit and not because you really figured it out. Are you sure that's what you want to do?"

"I was. Do you really think I'm only trying to please you?"

"Yes."

"Would that be so wrong?"

"Yes, you must do it for yourself, not me."

"But I love you."

"You shouldn't."

"Are we back to that again? I thought the other night changed all that."

"Not exactly."

"I think you have the idea that if you have a nice profession of some kind, I would be happy just being a housewife."

"More or less, yes."

"I want to sing."

" What's wrong with that?"

"I have a job offer with a band in Chicago right now."

"Chicago again?"

"yes."

"You can't be married to me and sing in Chicago, is that it?"

"I didn't tell you I am engaged to the guy who owns the band."

"And you can't get the job unless you go through with the engagement?"

"Uh huh. I don't see how I can keep from it."

"And yet you love me."

"Is that impossible to believe?"

"It doesn't make any sense to me, but if you have to do it and it's what you want how can I stop you?"

"You're not hurt?"

"Not hurt? Of course, I'm hurt. I could tear up houses and knock down trees, but it would not help. I cannot make you stay. I love you and I'm helpless." After a long pause, "If it doesn't work out, I'll still be here.

"You're very understanding."

"No. I'm just tired and out of ideas," I said. I knew you were not leaving until June. Things could change before then. There was still some time.

CHAPTER 13

"SHE'S ASLEEP"

I said I would call at 5:30 PM. It was 5:30 now.

"Hello," I said onto the phone.

"Hello," someone said back.

"Is the Princess there?" I asked.

"She's sleeping."

"Oh....Well, I'll call back."

At 6:00 I called again. You were still sleeping. Your sister said she would have you call when you woke up.

6:40. The phone rang. It was your sister sounding very frightened.

"What?"

"We can't wake her. She is unconscious, or something. We called a doctor."

"I'll be right over." I was stunned. I put on more presentable clothes and raced to your house. It was only a mile, but it took forever. I arrived and was led to your room. The doctor was not there yet. Working at the hospital I had taken some nurse's training. "Check the pulse, respiration, and temperature. Keep the patient warm. Keep everything as normal as possible."

You were lying atop the bed in your bathrobe. Your hair was in pin curls. Your face was quiet and serene. You looked quietly at peace, almost un-alive. My heart pounded. I was shaking. I turned to your mother, "Have you checked her pulse?"

"I can't find it."

"Have you got a thermometer?"

"Yes."

"Get it."

"You can't take her temperature by mouth. She's unconscious."

"Take it rectally," I said counting the pulse. She went for the thermometer. Your pulse was 56. Normal for you would be 80 to 90. Danger below 40. Pulse is OK. For the moment. I checked the respiration 16. 20 is normal, still OK. Your mother came with the thermometer. I slapped your face for a response. nothing. Twice more drew a wince but no more. The thermometer read 97.8. slightly low, but still quite safe. All in all, it did not seem to me that you were critical at this point.

"The doctor is here," someone said.

I told him what I had found, and he checked your pupils, never acknowledging that I was there but taking it all in, nevertheless. I could see when he looked into your eyes that your pupils were dilated. He asked if you had taken sleeping pills. Your mother said you had not and would not have because you had to work tonight. I could see he did not believe you had not taken some kind of sedative. He asked if you had ever used them. Your sister said, yes, you had had some, but they got thrown out. The doctor slapped your face as he listened. No response. He ran his finger up the length of your bare foot.no reflex. He tried again. Your leg moved. He reached in his bag for his blood pressure manometer. I watched

him strap it on your arm and squeeze the little bulb.
By watching the mercury bubble, I could see the reading was 90 over 60.low but not dangerous. The doctor put everything back in his bag then took out a syringe and injected the contents into your arm.

"We have to get her to the hospital for a stomach wash," he said.

"Can we take her in the car?" your mother asked, wanting to avoid the expense of an ambulance.

"We can use my car. The seat folds down flat," I offered.

"That should do. I'll meet you there," the doctor said leaving.

"The General or the Memorial?" I asked as the doctor as he went out.

"The General. Memorial is full."
After rolling you in a blanket your father and I navigated you through the house and into the passenger side of my car.

At the Emergency entrance I carried you from the car to the gurney where two nurses wheeled you into the emergency room. I helped move you from the gurney to the table. They asked me to wait outside. Your mother was there, and we waited in the waiting room smoking cigarettes. I ran out and fished in my pocket for change for the vending machine, but only found twenty-three cents. I needed a quarter. I asked the receptionist at the desk if she could spare 2 cents. I gave her my change and she gave me a quarter. I was too distracted to even be embarrassed.

"I wonder if she did it on purpose," your mother mused out loud in my direction, as if she thought I might know the answer.

"I don't know."

"You shouldn't get too emotionally involved with her. I don't want you to get hurt."

"I appreciate your concern for me, but I want to help her. I just cannot walk away. If I get hurt...that is a risk I'll have to take."

"You are much too good for her."

"Pooh, I have to disagree. I don't believe that."

"You don't really know about her."

"We have talked. She tells me she is bad. I do not care about any of that, whatever it is. I love her."

"Well, we appreciate what you have done. You seem to be the only one she listens to. She won't listen to any of us."

Just then there was as strange sound coming down the hall, like maybe a baby crying. I walked down the hall to get closer. I was startled to discover it was from your room. It must be you. I struggled to visualize you making that sound. It was painful to listen to. I finally did not want to hear it anymore and went back to your mother who was now walking toward me.

"It's her. There is no point in going down there. You can't see anything." I walked her back to the waiting room.

"I hope she's alright."

"Sure, she is."

"I hope it was an accident. We can't collect on the insurance if it wasn't."

"We'll just have to wait and see," I said.
We waited until they finally moved you to a private room. I followed the doctor into the room.

"Do you suppose I could stay here with her?" I asked the doctor.

"I don't think that will be necessary. She probably won't wake up until morning.

Why don't you go home and get some sleep?"

"I suppose you're right, but I want to be here if she does wake up. I work nights and I slept all day and have taken the night off anyway. I can stay in the waiting room if I can't stay in here."

"Talk to the nurse and see what she says."

"OK."

There was only you and I and the doctor in the room. I do not know where your mother went. Suddenly you wretched to vomit and the doctor grabbed for a kidney pan and held your head over the edge of the bed. You were still asleep. The doctor said your blood pressure was now up to 100 over 70 and you would be alright. He then asked me what I knew of the situation leading up to this. I told him you had bad dreams, that we both did. I told him everything I thought was pertinent. He seemed extremely interested in the dreams. He said he wanted to talk further about them. Just then your mother entered the room. He told her there was nothing that could be done until morning. Everything would be alright. I offered to take your mother home and she accepted.

"There's nothing we can do here, I guess," she said, and we left.

CHAPTER 14

ABOUT CHICAGO

Your little brother and little sister were in bed. Your big sister had left for the city. She had to drive the fifty miles alone and perform alone as well. I was concerned about her driving. She was pretty shaken by the day's events. Your mother and father and I drank coffee and talked about you. Your father seemed the least disturbed outwardly, but I could feel his deep concern. The three of us must have consumed four cups of coffee apiece. Eventually Chicago came up. Your mother said that when she visited you there last year you had been depressed...almost to the point of doing what you had just done. Then she said you met a musician. He had been genuinely nice to you. "She seemed to come to life after that."

"What sort of guy is he?" I asked.

"I don't like him," your father said.

"But, dear, you don't even know him."

"I still don't like him."

"Do you think she was really in love with him?" I heard myself asking.

"I think she thought she was," your mother answered.

"Of course, if she was depressed and he came along and was nice to her she may very well think she was in love with him." I heard myself talking and was startled by the way that description would fit me as well.

"Listen, we have a tape recording he sent to her last month. Would you like to hear it?" It was your father this time.

"Yes, I would."

One side of the tape was music and the other side a conversation between the musician and his mother while she was in the kitchen preparing dinner. There were asides to a cat which was also waiting to be fed. He sounded about thirty, leader of an orchestra, did not mow lawns, lived with his mother and the cat. He sounded temperamental and only had little to say about you except you were beautiful and had been a great help with the dishes. The picture of him created by this tape was not particularly good. Turning to your father, I said, "I don't like him either."

Looking at the clock on the mantel I saw it was eleven o'clock. "I'm going back to the hospital," I said.

"The doctor said there was no need," your mother offered.

"By the way," your father began. "I was going through her purse looking for any kind of sleeping pills and I found this letter. It is from you dated way back in June. Do you want to read it?"

"My letter? I did not know she had kept it. Yes, I would like to read it. I cannot remember all that I said. Maybe it will shed some light." I read the letter:

"Dear Princess, I have wanted to write this letter for some time, years actually. I wrote a draft last week but tore it up. I will try again. I am at work. I work at a hospital for the mentally impaired. I am working nights so I can attend college in the daytime. The work is interesting, and I like it. Last year I went to a college in Utah on a scholarship. This year I am attending the local Junior College. I am taking required courses still and am thinking about pre-med.

I cannot tell you in a letter how much it meant to me to paint the portrait of you that I sold to your mother. I really did not want to part with it. It was as though I had touched you and knew you in a very personal way that formed an attachment that somehow connected us. I fancied myself in love with you, but I have felt that way since the first time I saw you in junior high school. You seemed quiet and unapproachable then. I never had the courage to walk up to you and say anything. You were so beautiful and always surrounded by your girlfriends. I had nothing to say to you except to tell you how pretty you were and that I adored you. After that I would have been speechless and would have looked like an idiot. If you were to have made fun of me, I would have died. Eventually high school was over, and we went our separate ways,

I to college, and you and your sister off dancing in clubs all over the country.

When I recently stopped to see your parents and they gave me your address, I was so excited I could hardly sleep. At last, I can unbind my heart and let my feelings flow. I have nothing to lose. The worst that can happen is that you won't answer, but at least I have spoken my heart and have felt a burden lifted.

I just finished writing a speech for speech class. The title was: WHY ARE YOU WHAT YOU ARE? The body of the speech tells how the need for feeling important can lead us into dishonest thinking and frustration. The need is present in everyone; how they handle it is the important factor. Here is the closing paragraph: 'When I say develop your own individuality, I mean develop the potential within you. I do not know what your potentials are...that is something you must find out for yourself, but in looking, don't kid yourself into thinking you are something you are not. Have faith in yourself but be honest enough to admit your own limitations. Above all, do not try to fit someone else's pattern. For even if you succeed you will only be a copy.

We are all born different. Do not try to be like someone else. We all have the opportunity to develop ourselves. That is the greatest thing we can contribute to the world. Do not sell yourself short. If you can do that, develop your own potential, then people are not likely to look and ask, 'Why are you what you are?' no more than they would ask the sun or the moon. They will see, like the sun and the moon, you are what you must be.
All my love,"

When I finished reading, I gave it back to your father and left for the hospital.

CHAPTER 15

"I DON'T WANT TO GO HOME"

At the hospital I found your room and tapped on the door. The Special Nurse came to the door and softly inquired what I wanted. I told her I was going to wait all night, and I would like to wait in the room if I could. She said she did not think I would be allowed in the room, but she would ask the Charge Nurse. The nursing office was across the hall behind me and I turned to find the Charge Nurse standing there listening to the whole conversation. She said it was up to the Special Nurse to decide. The Special Nurse then decided I should wait in the waiting room since doctor's orders were: 'The patient should be kept quiet.' I decided the best thing to do was just go to the waiting room. "Will you let me know if she wakes up?" I asked.

"Yes," she said, adding, "You may come and check as often as you like."

I checked every half hour. At 2:30 AM. I went to check and heard sobbing inside. I wanted to open the door and be beside you, but just tapped on the door instead. The door was not latched, and my tapping opened it a crack and I could see the nurse motion me to stay out and shut the door. She came over and said you were sobbing but you were still not awake. She said you mumbled something now and then about not being any good. I really wanted to be near you but had to go back to the waiting room.

At 3:10 AM I saw the nurse coming down the hall. She beckoned to me with her finger to come. My heart started pounding. As we walked toward your room, she told me you were awake and asking for me. She said you were groggy and could not see anything yet.

Standing beside you, I grasped your hand and looked down at your helpless face. I did not know what to say. You squeezed my hand very tightly and said something I could not hear. I thought you said, "Why didn't you call?"
"I did call," I said hoping I had heard correctly.

"You were too busy," you whispered. You turned your head in a writhing motion and let go of my hand. You started sobbing again and mumbled things I could not hear. I felt suddenly that I was to blame for all this. At least you seemed to think so. I wondered if I had said I would call and had forgotten to do it. I could not remember, even now, if that were true or not. I felt very guilty. The nurse asked me to leave. She would call me again later. While I waited, the nurse brought me some coffee.

At 3:55 AM the Special Nurse came for me. You wanted to see me again. You were sitting and you were smiling at me as I entered the room. I forgot about feeling guilty. Your pupils were still dilated, and I was sure you could not see me, but you knew I was there. I stood beside you and gave you my hand which you took with both of yours and pulled it to your cheek. You touched it against your face and smiled. I felt much better.

"I love you," you tried to say. Your lips moved, but no sound came out. I knew what you said. I could feel it.

"I love you too," I said.

"I wanted to call you," you articulated without sound.

"Why didn't you?"

"You were busy doing something with your brother."

"No, I wasn't. Even if I had been, I would have come."

"I didn't want to bother you."

"Promise me that if you ever need me, you'll call next time."

"OK." You sounded really exhausted.

"You better get some rest now."

"When am I going home?"

"Maybe in the morning."

"What time is it now?"

"Four o'clock in the morning."

"I don't want to go home," you started to sob.

"OK. It's alright. Where do you want to go?"

"With you."

I realized there were other voices in the room. Your mother and sister were there. I wished they had not come just now. I did not think you wanted to see them. I could not very well tell them to go away.

"Hi," your sister said. You did not answer, just nodded. I sensed you did not want to talk to them. I wondered if they were not part of what you were trying to get away from. You cut them short every time they spoke, or you just did not bother to answer at all. In this half-stuporous condition you made no effort to hide your feelings. I interjected that I thought you needed to get some sleep. I started moving toward the door and they began to follow. I said I would stay in the waiting room and call them if anything developed by morning. Once they left, I returned to your room.

"They're gone," I said.

"All of them?"

"All but me."

"You should go home and get some sleep."

"I can't sleep. I want to stay. Anyway, I slept all day and I'm supposed to be up all night."

"I love you," you said.

"I love you too," I said back. I stayed with you, not saying much, until almost five o'clock.

"I shouldn't be here. I should be dead," you said in a barely audible voice.

"Why? Don't talk like that."

"Are you angry with me?"

"I could never be angry with you." You squeezed my hand to your cheek and I just stayed there until you dozed off to sleep. You were smiling in slumber when I left the room. I told the nurse I was going for a walk around the block.

CHAPTER 16

BACK HOME

Outside the night air was growing thick with morning fog. It was cold and refreshing. I was glad I had worn my jacket. The day was beginning and all around were the busy sounds of a new day. Faint sounds and muffled by the soft fog. I felt that a crisis had passed but could not imagine what this day would bring. Taking you home to my folks' house could only be a temporary solution. We lived in a two-room tar paper shack. Your folks' house was a lovely, sprawling home with many rooms and those huge picture windows. This is oil and water, I thought. Well, one step at a time.

You slept soundly. Your mother came at 8:00 o'clock to relieve me.

"You better go home and get some sleep," she said.

"I think I'll try." I was exhausted. I went home.

It was Sunday morning. No one was up when I got home. Mother heard me and came to ask how you were doing. I went over the high spots briefly. I did not want to go into all the details. We drank coffee together, and then I slipped into bed.

I could not sleep. I just laid there tossing. I was in a very tense state of mind. I felt I should be near you back at the hospital. After an hour I gave up trying to sleep. I got up, dressed, shaved, and tried to eat something, but I was not hungry. The phone rang. It was your father. He said they were bringing you home from the hospital. I said I would be over shortly.

You were not yet there when I arrived. We drank coffee while we waited. Our conversation revealed nothing new. I told him about the night at the hospital, leaving out what I thought best. It seemed forever before you finally arrived.

I helped you from the car to the house and then to your bedroom. You were still groggy and a bit wobbly. You did not say anything as we went through the house. I helped you get comfortable in the bed and covered you up. You smiled.

"How do you feel?" I asked.

"Woozy," you smiled.

"Can you see yet?"

"Yes. A little. I can see your eyes...only there are three of them." You articulated each word slowly and carefully. You looked better. I almost felt I could relax.

"Wanna try for four?" I said, keeping things light.

"No. Three's enough."

"Is your stomach sore?"

"A little. Why?"

"Well, when they pump your stomach it can be a bit sore."

"Did they do that?"

"Yes."

"Can I have a cigarette?"

I lit us both one and we relaxed a bit. You raised up and looked at yourself in the mirror over your dressing table.

"Ooh! Look at my hair!"

"Well, you're not at a party, you're in bed."

"Have you been to bed yet?"

"I tried...couldn't sleep."

"Why don't you pull that little bed up next to mine and get some sleep?"

I did as you suggested and looked around to see if any of the family could see me. The door was nearly closed. No one was there, so I closed it and laid down next to you.

"May I kiss you?" I asked. You moved toward me and closed your eyes. After a pleasant silence I decided it was alright to ask the question I needed to have answered.

"Why did you do it?"

"I'm not sure." You spoke without emotion, but your words were clear now.

"Did you do it on purpose?"

"Sort of...I was tired. I was only going to take one to go to sleep. I took it and found myself counting the rest in the box. There were seven left. I wondered if it would hurt. I took another. I began to think how nice it would be to just go to sleep and not wake up to all the noise. It seemed so peaceful not to wake up.

Nothing could bother me then. No more dreams. I took another. I felt nothing. I kept thinking how quiet and peaceful it would be. I took two more. I began to feel drowsy. I wondered if I really wanted to do it. I looked at the box. There were four left. I picked one up and looked at it. I was getting sleepy. Someone tapped on the door. I swallowed the pill in my hand and slipped the box under my pillow. My little sister came in and asked what I was doing. I told her I was sleepy and to go out. She left. I went to sleep and don't remember anything after that. Why didn't they let me sleep? It was so peaceful. It was nice. It did not hurt. I just went to sleep and did not feel anything. Why did they wake me up?"

"If you ever feel like doing that again, please talk to me first," I said.

"I shouldn't be here," you said, starting to sob.
I held you close, searching my mind for something to say.

"Did you read FROM HERE TO ETERNITY?" I finally asked.

"Yes."

Remember the guy who shot himself?"

"Yes."

"He didn't really mean to do it. Remember? After it was too late, he wished he had not done it, remember?"

"I kind of felt like that, but it didn't hurt, and it was nice."

"Don't talk that way. I love you. Doesn't that mean anything to you?"

"Yes. I'm sorry if I hurt you, but I told you you'd get hurt."

"Don't you love me?"

"Yes."

"Don't you think we could be happy?"

"Yes...maybe."

"Well, give me a chance to show your life is worthwhile. Is that asking too much?"

"I guess not."

Suddenly bolting upright in bed, you said, "I want to get up." There was fear in your eyes; they were wide and fixed. I was scared. I did not think you could walk, and I forced you back onto the bed. I held you for several minutes before you stopped struggling. You did not seem to be struggling against me, but against the whole house. You seemed to look clear through me into the wall. Finally, you relaxed and started sobbing again. When you stopped you looked at me and recognized me again. You clutched me tightly as if I were protecting you from something. I moved my fingers up and down your back, gently. You relaxed and smiled at me.

"I love you," you said.

"I love you too," I said.

"I love you so much. Don't leave me."

I kissed you and laid back to try to get some rest. I needed sleep, but I could not trust myself to go to sleep with you this unpredictable.

"Do you still see three eyes?" I asked just to be talking.

"Uh huh."

"I guess we'll just have to live with it,"

"Why don't you get some sleep?"

"I'll try," I lied. I stretched out and pretended to go to sleep.

"I thought you had to work last night." You forgot I was supposed to be sleeping.

"I called off. I Don't have to be back 'til Thursday. I have three days off."

"You're off until Thursday?"

"Uh huh."

"You going to stay with me until Thursday?"

"If you want."

"I do. Yes, I do."

"OK. I'll have to check and see if it's alright with your folks."

"They won't mind."

"Where will I sleep?"

"Right there where you are now."

"Right here by you?"

"Yes, why not?"

"That should be interesting." I said slyly, partly in fun, partly serious. I could not help but smile to myself. Just then your father came in with a tray of coffee and cream and sugar.

"Anyone want some coffee?"

"Smells good," I said.

"How's my baby?" he said in an almost sincere voice. I knew he was more concerned than he let on. He seemed to me to have stronger feeling for you than he was able to demonstrate. He was suffering quietly, it seemed to me. I began thinking about your relationship. He was not your real father. You had different last names. You and your older sister had the same last name, but the two young ones had his name. Your mother must have had you and your sister between 1932 and 1935. You would have been around nine or ten when the second world war started. Your half brother and sister were 12 and 15, both born about the time the war was over. Your father (stepfather) mentioned to me that he was retired from the navy. He must have married your mother at the end of the war. My ruminating was interrupted.

"Better," you answered.

I sensed a wall between you and your father. You both played at loving each other and paid some lip service to it, but it was not satisfying either of you. He left as quietly as he came in, closing the door behind him.

CHAPTER 17

RUNAWAY

We passed the day in your bedroom, just lying there. Occasionally someone brought in coffee or some food; otherwise, we were alone. Nothing happened until dusk.

The small lamp on the dresser was broken. It was not yet dark enough to turn on the overhead light. The room was dim and shadowy.

"Turn on the hall light," you pleaded.

"Sure."

I got up and went to the door, opened it, and reached around the corner for the switch. I found it and flicked it on with my fingers. The light leaked into the room through the crack of the door I left ajar. I laid back down on the bed.

"Did you have a bad dream?"

"No."

"Why are you afraid of the dark."

"I don't know." As if the words started it, you bolted in the bed. I tried to pull you down, but you were determined to get up.

"Let me go outside!"

"It's cold out there. You need to get more rest." Your eyes had that wild look again. The darkness, despite the hall light seemed to terrify you. I jumped up and turned on the overhead light hoping that would calm you. It did not.

"I have to get outside. I can't stand it in here!"

"Alright, we'll take a walk. Wait till I get your robe." It was no good trying to restrain you.

The best thing to do was humor you until you calmed down. At least, that seemed the best thing to do at the moment.

"You won't run away, will you?"

"I want to take a walk," you said not hearing me.

"Alright, lean on me. I'll help you out." We went through the house. No one said anything and pretended not to notice us. The air outside was cold. The moon was full, and the sky was clear. I let go of you so you could stand on your feet. You took off running. I ran after you. I was taken by surprise and you almost ran the two hundred feet to the road before I caught up to you. You were terribly disturbed, and it was an effort to hold you.

"Let me go!"

"I can't. What if a car comes along?"

"I want to be alone. Let me walk by myself."

"Where do you want to go?"

"I don't know. I just want to walk by myself. Let me go!"

"No. I can't. Don't you understand? I want you to do what you want, but I cannot take a chance on you getting hurt. Please, don't fight me."

You were very agitated and tried to break away again. There was a bench by the road. It was for a bus stop, I think. I tried to get you to walk over to it, but you would not go. I finally picked you up and carried you to it. You fought and kicked all the way, but I got there and sat you down. You started crying. I had to hold you down. You were completely hysterical.

"What are you so afraid of?" I asked. No answer. I shook you. No effect. I slapped your face. No response. I slapped harder. You snapped out of it. I was sorry I hit you so hard. It had to hurt. You sat there holding your hand against your cheek and looking at me as if you could not figure out why I hit you. You did not seem angry. Just puzzled.

"We'd better go in now," I said rather apologetically.

You did not answer, just got up and started walking toward the house. Your folks asked how you were as we went through the house to your room. You answered in a kind of hypnotic voice that you were alright. I beckoned your older sister to follow us. I asked her if she would stay with you while I called the doctor. I was really shaking now. I knew I needed help. I could not risk my going to sleep with you acting so unpredictably.

CHAPTER 18

DREAM TALK

"Hello, Doc. She is very depressed and agitated.... tried to run away."

"I'll be there in half an hour." he hung up. It was 8:30 in the evening; he would be here by 9:00 o'clock. I had some coffee and waited. I drank the cup of coffee in three gulps. I did not intend to drink it so fast. I seemed to have only one speed and it was full ahead. I took a cup of coffee in for you and motioned for your sister to leave us alone.

"I called the doctor."

"Why?"

"I want him to see you."

"What kind of doctor?" you asked suspiciously.

"Not what you're thinking. The same doctor that took care of you at the hospital."

"He's not a ...."

"No. He's just an MD."

"But I'm alright. I don't need a doctor."

"Look Princess, I haven't slept for over thirty hours."

"I know, I'm sorry. You should have slept."

"How could I? The only way I can sleep is for you to let the doctor see you."

"Tell him not to come."

"You don't need to be afraid of him."

"I don't want to see him. Tell him not to come."

"Forgive me, but he is coming, and you will see him, and there's nothing you can do about it now." You seemed so lucid and in control of yourself, I wondered if maybe you did not need to see the doctor. We waited. The doctor was on time.

The doctor was disarmingly kind and you began to relax. After a bit he asked if you were still having bad dreams. You were surprised by the question, "How do you know about the dreams?" You were on guard.

"He told me," the doctor pointed toward me.

"Oh..." you seemed to decide it was OK.

"Would you like to tell me about it?" he asked almost casually.

"It's kind of silly."

"Everyone thinks their dreams are silly. I would still like to hear about it."

You recited the dream. He was very attentive, and you appeared a bit less tense having shared it with a stranger.

"What does it mean?" you were very eager to hear some explanation.

The doctor stayed for almost an hour. He posed the question to you as to what your true feelings were about your mother and sister. He suggested you might have some feelings about them that you were unwilling to admit. That when you begin to feel tense maybe you should go out and break some bottles. He thought you might be resentful about being forced into dancing to satisfy your mother's ambition rather than your own. You had freely admitted you hated dancing, but you could not admit your resentment toward those who pushed you into it. He also suggested that since your mother had such high ideals and moral values that, rather than saying you were angry with her, you broke those rules in a subconscious effort to express yourself. You could not refuse to dance but you could disobey the rules of conduct and plead helplessness. It was not your fault; you were just "no good." He finished by saying it would take time for you to sort all that out, but you could do it. You had a smile on your face when he left.

"Thank you for coming," you said. "I'm sorry if we wasted your time." You sounded a tiny bit sarcastic but completely rational. I felt I could risk going to sleep now. I said I had to go call my mother to say I would be staying here for the night and went into the living room in time to hear the doctor. "She'll be alright for now," he said.

"What about the dreams?" your mother queried.

"They seem to be the result of great anxiety that probably goes way back to her childhood and it will take time for her to figure out. Much of it she will have to work out for herself. No amount of telling her will be believed. She is not ready just yet.

"I suppose I'm to blame," your mother said sounding like a martyr. She was sincere and I felt sorry for her.

"To be perfectly frank, yes, you are partly responsible."

"I shouldn't have made her dance."

"No, you shouldn't have."

"I'll tell her to stop."

"That's the very thing you should not do," the doctor said. "I mean, now is the time to start treating her like she is her own person. Let her make up her own mind about what she wants to do. Do not tell her anything. Make her feel she has a perfect right to do whatever she pleases."

"What should we do about last night?" your father asked.

"Nothing. If she wants to talk about it, listen. If she does not want to talk about it, do not. She may start to talk about it and stop. Do not press her. She feels guilty enough. Do not add to it. I think you should let the young man take care of her; he seems to have a fairly good sense of what to do. He'll know to call me if it's necessary."

"What about the pills?" your mother asked.

"Oh, yes, I have a prescription here for a sedative and another for when she feels a little blue. Do not worry about the sedative. It is a new kind of sleeping pill. If she takes one, she will feel drowsy. If she takes two, she will feel nauseated. If she takes three, she will vomit. The other pills are just when she is feeling a little dejected. Is that all clear?"

"Yes, I think so," everyone said together.

"Well, everything is under control. I will be going now. Goodnight." He went out the door and into the night.

I returned to your bedroom after calling my mother and explaining I would be staying the night. I left the door ajar, climbed into the little bed next to yours, kissed you and fell into a much-needed sleep. Once during the night, I imagined that you had crawled into my bed and snuggled, but there was no sign of that having happened. When I finally woke up you were standing over me with a cup of coffee and looking down with a smile.

"Here's some coffee." The cup was hot. I struggled and sat up.

"Well, you're all bright and cheerful."

"Mm... I feel good."

I was refreshed with a new day and having slept. Yesterday was only a memory. You were standing there as beautiful as ever and I could only say," I love you."

"Me too…. I mean you," you said sitting down on the edge of the little bed.

"I guess turnabout is fair play."

"I suppose so, but what do you mean?"

"Well, yesterday I took care of you, now you are taking care of me."

"I like to take care of you. You look like a little boy in the morning. Your hair and everything remind me of a little boy."

"I must look messed up and slept in."

"I like it. Are just going to lie around all day or are you going to get up?"

"I'm considering getting up. There is no hurry. I'm not going anywhere."

"I thought we had a date tonight," you said.

"We do but that's tonight...it's still daytime. By the way, where would you like to go?"

"I don't care."

"How about driving to the coast and watch the moon light up the ocean?"

"Yes, I like the water."

"Good, we'll leave around seven. OK?"

"Fine."

You went out and I dressed. You seemed to be in good spirits. I decided you would be alright for a while and I could go home and get some food and rest. You should be alright until I got back.

CHAPTER 19

MOONLIGHT AND SAND

t seven o'clock I was dressed in casual slacks and a sport shirt knocking at your door. I had some flowers in one hand hoping you would be pleasantly surprised.

"Come on in," someone said from inside where they sat.

"I opened the door and went in. Something was wrong. Everyone sat there looking dejected. My first thought was that someone had taken you away somewhere. I searched the room for you, but you were not there. I was afraid to ask where you were. I thought surely someone would speak up. I was afraid to find out.

"Our bird has flown the coup," your mother said.

"What?" I said astonished.

"She's gone," your sister put in.

"Well, where?"

"Who knows," your mother answered. "She left about an hour ago."

"I thought we had a date," I muttered foolishly.

"I know," your sister said. "I told her she should call you, but she didn't want to."

"She just wants to hurt you," your mother said to me.

"And you have no idea where she went?"

"She went to get drunk," your mother denounced. "I have no idea where."

I left. I had no idea where you might be, but I would find you. I was very worried and more than a little hurt. Why had you done this? I stopped at every bar I thought you might be in. I found you in less than half an hour sitting on a stool by yourself in a quiet bar. I had been in this bar many times by myself. I walked over and sat on the stool next to you. I was shaking. I did not know how you would react to my finding you. I just sat there waiting until you turned your head and said, "How did you find me?"

"It wasn't hard."

"You must really be a mind reader; you always know what I'm going to do."

"Are you angry that I found you?"

"No, a little surprised, but not angry."

"Why didn't you call me? We had a date, didn't we?"

"Yes, we had a date, but I didn't call because I didn't think you would want to get drunk. And I did not want you to see me this way. Now are you convinced that I'm bad?"

"I have been considering getting drunk myself. As far as my thinking you are bad...you sure are going out of your way to try to prove it. You are failing, but I suppose you will keep trying. Do you want me to leave?"

"No, I'm glad you came."

"So am I."

"Are you hurt because I didn't call you?"

"No," I lied.

"How can you be so understanding?"

"I'm not. I'm really just stubborn." I ordered a Vodka Collins.

"I love you," you whispered in my ear.

"I love you too."

"I'm getting high," you smirked.

"I lied to you," I said seriously. The bartender brought another drink. I fished for money in my pocket and was aware you were looking at me. I did not look back until I put the change away.

"What do you mean, you lied to me?"

"When I said I wasn't hurt when you didn't call. I lied. Every time I have said you could not hurt me. I lied. It hurt a lot."

"I warned you would get hurt. You just wouldn't listen."

"I didn't think you would try so hard. Why do you feel so compelled to make me believe you are no good? You can keep trying but you will not convince me you are no good. You will be wasting your time." We hashed the pros and cons of good and bad as only two alcohol stimulated intellects can do, reaching no absolute or remembered conclusion before heading out to see the moon light up the Pacific Ocean. It was twenty foggy miles, but I drove slowly, mindful of my precious cargo. Everything was alright for now.

The fog was oddly not thick as we reached the coast. For the last half mile there was no fog at all. I drove down a narrow peninsula that jutted out into the water for almost two miles. The road was paved to the end. The peninsula was roughly one hundred yards wide. On one side was the ocean, the other the bay. About two miles up the coastline a long finger of land poked out into the sea in an irregular arc. The peninsula I was driving on shot out into the water and almost met the end of the other peninsula. The area inside the two arcs composed the bay nearly a mile square. Off to the right I could see the bay and its calm shoreline. To the left pounded the ocean surf. The ground on either side of the road was sand interspersed with weed-like vegetation and a kind of brush resembling sagebrush. The ground was just rolling sand. I decided to try to drive off the road toward the ocean side. Perhaps the alcohol impaired my judgment. It must have. I do not think I would have attempted to drive out on the sand if I had not been drinking. I left the road and drove toward the surf at a slow even speed. In front of me was a low crest of sand. To see the surf, I would have to cross that rise or at least sit atop it. It was not a steep incline, only perhaps five feet high but gradual. The crest was about a hundred feet from the road. I traveled three quarters of the distance when I felt the front wheels bog down. I immediately stopped and began to back up. I went maybe ten feet and stopped, thinking I was now safe. I was about to turn off the key and park when I decided I should back up a bit more. I engaged the clutch and felt the wheels spinning. I jockeyed forward and backward trying to get momentum. The more I tried, the deeper I went into the sand. I got out to look. It was no use. The sand was up to the rear axle. I got back into the car and turned off the motor.

"Is it bad?" you asked, sounding not very worried.

"Pretty bad. Up to the axle. I might be able to jack it up and put brush and rocks under the wheels for traction. For now, let's just relax. I'm in no hurry to go anywhere."

"Don't you have to work tomorrow?"

"No, I'm off 'til Thursday; it's only Tuesday."

"Good."

"I reached down, pulled the levers and lowered the seats until they were almost flat. We stretched out and listened to the soft music and looked at the moon. The moon hung like a lantern and lit up the shoreline on either side of the peninsula. I could see cows grazing along the shoreline down toward the end of the strip of sand.

"Mm....it's nice here," you said, still feeling the drinks.

"Are you cold?" I asked.

"A little."

I got two blankets from the trunk of the car and spread them over us. We were going to be here for a while, might as well be warm.

"I'm almost glad we got stuck," I said.

"Me too. I'm glad you came and found me tonight."

"So am I."

"I love you," you said, feeling the drinks but sounding like you meant it.

It was good being here with you so relaxed. I was glad you were a bit drunk, not sloppy, just warm, and pleasant. In the moonlight I looked into your eyes and was completely engulfed by your beauty. The alcohol had removed your inhibitions and you seemed willing to talk about anything. As I lay there, I suddenly looked up and saw the sun visor, which reminded me I had slipped a small package behind there. I reached up and retrieved it.

"I have something for you," I said. "Close your eyes." I took your arm and put the bracelet on it. You opened your eyes when you felt it touch your skin.

"Oh, it's beautiful. Why did you do that? When did you get it?"

"I've had it for almost a month. I had been going to give it to you right along, but I kept forgetting to take it when I left the house. Tonight, I remembered."

"But what's it for? I mean why?"

"Call it a birthday present if you like. I bought it from a friend who makes them. This one was so nice I could not resist. I had to buy it for you. Do you like it?"

"Oh, yes, it's beautiful."

The bracelet was not that expensive, but it was pretty. It had three rows of stones side by side in each link. The moon shimmered through the prisms of the cut stones producing every color in the spectrum. No matter how you held it in the light it was dazzling. It was perfect on you.

"I'm glad you like it."

Instead of answering you kissed me. After a while I decided to see what I could do to get unstuck from the sand. You offered to help but I said there was nothing you could do. "You stay in the car and stay warm," I said. The ocean air was cold outside the car.

I took the jack from the trunk of the car and jacked up the back end which had sunk into the sand. I stuffed brush and rocks under the wheels, let the jack down and got into the car.

"Is it fixed?"

"I'm about to find out.' I started the engine and engaged the clutch slowly. The car moved two feet and went down again into the sand,

"Where are you going?"

"I'm going to try again." I repeated the process with the same results. I thought I might be able to inch my way to the road but for the fact that every time I moved. I was veering off to the right, and if I continued, I would go in a circle and never get to the road.

"No luck?"

"No luck."

"I don't want to go home anyway," you said half-serious.

"I'm all for not going home but I have to go to work in a couple of days. Besides, I have no money and don't get paid until next week."

"When I'm with you I forget about everything else. I'm almost afraid to be alone with you because you make me want to give up all the things I want and just be with you."

"Why be afraid of that? There's nothing to fear."

"But I don't want to give up those things."

"Who said you had to?"

"Won't I?"

"I don't see why."

"Well, if we got married how could I do those things?"

"Just do them. You could still sing if you get married."

"But if I sing, I will be traveling all around. You cannot take your job with you. You have to stay in one place, and we wouldn't be together."

"Well, I hadn't really thought of that. I do not know the answer to that. There has to be a way to solve that problem." I was stumped.

"Any way, we're here for the night so let's just enjoy it," you said.

We snuggled in the blankets and went to sleep holding each other and were happy for here and now.

CHAPTER 20

THE RESCUE

The sun was bright, the sky clear and the air crisp when I woke up. You were still asleep. I sat up and looked down at you. How nice it was to wake up next to you. To look at your beautiful face sent a thrill all through me. I wanted to paint you from life, looking at you. I could not believe you loved me, but here you were beside me stuck in the sand at sunup and no way to go anywhere. We were going to have to deal with that very soon.

"Wake up, sleepy head."

"Hi," you squinted.

"How do you feel this fine day?"

"Fine."

"Are you hungry?"

"I'd like some coffee."

"The only thing we have is some soup in a can and nothing to open it with except a jack handle."

"I don't want any soup."

"Good. I don't think I could open it with a jack handle anyway."

"What shall we do?"

"I think we might better try to get to town. We'll have to walk." The closest town was about five miles by the road. We could make it out just the other side of the bay. We would have to walk all the way down the road and then up the highway the rest of the distance. We managed a mile when a car came along headed for the end of the peninsula. I stopped the car and told the elderly lady who was driving that our car was stuck in the sand. I do not know what I expected her to do, but she was our immediate link to the rest of the world, and I figured she would have a suggestion. I saw past her that there was an older gentleman next to her and a younger person in the back seat.

"If you'll wait here until we come back from the point, we'll take you to a phone." She was very pleasant.

"We may get out of here yet." I said to you.

"I wonder what they think of us. Me standing here with my shoes in my hand. They must know we have been here all night. I hate to think what they must be thinking."

"You can't tell. They did seem nice though."

I could not imagine why they had to go down to the point. There was absolutely nothing down there but the ocean. No matter. I could see them coming back. They were alongside in a minute and we climbed into the back seat with the young man. We introduced ourselves, and they did likewise. They were easy people to like on short notice.

"We certainly appreciate this," I said.

"That's quite alright. I'll bet you're starved, aren't you," she said.

"Not so hungry, but we could sure use some coffee."

"Well, we have a little cabin just up the shore. Would you like to stop there for some coffee and a bite to eat?"

"We don't want to put you out. It sure sounds good though."

"That's just what we'll do then," the nice lady continued.

The cabin was cozy. We learned that they had built it themselves. The younger man was the son and had a serious heart condition which required him to spend his time leisurely. That was why they were here today, to just take things easy. The cabin had a large picture window facing the ocean. The view was grand.

"Nothing will be open in town for another hour, so you will have to wait here. When we go for the paper, we can take you to a phone so you can call the garage."

"Mm. This coffee is good," you said smiling at your hostess.

We talked of various things while we waited. We had more coffee and smoked some cigarettes. I told them I did not know how I could ever repay them for their kindness.

"Just pass it on," the husband said. "We have been in a few tough spots too. Someone always came along and helped. We are just paying back what we owe.

You can do the same thing someday and we'll be repaid."

I rode to town with the husband. You stayed where it was warm and waited for me to return since we would have to wait there for the tow truck anyway. In town I called the garage and explained what happened and where we were. They said they could be there in half an hour. You had made yourself quite at home, and you were talking amiably to the nice lady when her husband and I returned.

"You say you and your sister dance in the city?" the nice lady said.

"Yes, at the Regent Hotel in the Hawaiian Room," you replied.

"You do Hawaiian dancing?"

"Yes."

"You are Hawaiian?"

"Uh huh."

"You are certainly pretty. We'll have to stop in and catch the show some night," the husband put in.

"We're only scheduled for another week," you said.

"You must enjoy dancing," the nice lady said.

"As a matter of fact, I don't," you said with surprising frankness.

"Oh?"

"No. The only reason I do it is because my mother wanted me to."

"That's too bad. You said you danced with your sister. Does she like to dance?"

"Yes, she likes it. I'm the odd one."

"Well, what do you want to do?" It was the son who spoke.

"I want to be a singer," you said timidly.

"Well, why don't you sing then?" he went on.

"Because I have been too busy dancing, I guess. I don't know if really can sing anyway."

"I think you should give it a try. Find out," the husband said trying to be encouraging.

They went on talking while I stationed myself at the window looking for the truck. What a nice place to come and paint. The truck came into view.

"Here it is," I interrupted.

We said our goodbyes. The son gave me his card, and we left bathed in warm smiles.

The car came out easily. The truck driver attached a long cable to the bumper of the car, pushed a button and the cable wound up on the spool and the car was on solid roadway in no time.

"Did you pay him?" you asked.

"I have no money. He gave me a bill and I promised to mail him a check when I got home."

On the way home we met your father going the other way. We had not even given a thought to other people wondering where we were. Everyone was worried. The whole countryside was looking for us.

"I'll call my folks when we get to the next town and a phone," I said.

"Don't bother, just get home, I'll call them," your father said. He was not angry, just helpful. Nevertheless, we could not help feeling a little guilty for not having thought about other people's feelings. You moved closer and gripped my arm, making me feel we were both joined by our common guilt. We had both "goofed," but it was also a wonderful moment shared.

CHAPTER 21

AT MY HOUSE

I hope your folks are not angry because of me," you said.

"They won't be. You'll see," I was fairly sure. I took you straight home. We were not even through the door when your mother rushed to meet us. She said we had better try to find my folks. They were terribly worried about us. She said your father had called and told her he was unable to reach my parents.

"They must be out looking for you." Your mother seemed to be more worried about my family than her own. Of course, she already knew you were okay. We drove off to my house. There was no sense trying to chase them down, without a clue where to start. It would be best just to wait until they came home. While we waited, I called the Highway Patrol to see if anyone had turned in a call to look for us. They said your doctor had called to see if there were any accidents reported in the area. I thanked them and told them to tell anyone inquiring about us that we were at my parent's house. I then called your doctor to tell him we were alright. He said he was genuinely concerned because your mother called him thinking you might have tried to finish what you started on Sunday. He asked what shape you were in. I said you were fine. He said he wanted to talk about you, and I should come to his office at nine o'clock. I agreed and hung up.

"What did he say?" you asked.

"He just said, your mother called him. That is why he called the Highway Patrol. He wanted to see if there had been any accidents reported." I did not mention his wanting to see me at nine o'clock. We made some coffee and waited.

"Where are all your paintings?"

"All over the walls. I'll show you." I led you around the room. We only had two rooms. This one and my folks' bedroom. My bed was in the corner of this main room. The paintings were all here.

"This is a portrait of my father as a young man."

"He resembles you. Who's this one?"

"A girl I used to go with."

"And this?"

"A pastel of a bullfight not quite what I wanted, but I like it some."

"Oh, another bull fight."

"Yes, in oil. It took half the time of the pastel and I like it better. You can't tell by the time it takes how well things will come out.

"And here. Yet another bull fight, but big."

"Four by eight feet. That is done with ultraviolet paint. It glows under black light. I think I can sell that one."

"Why don't you?"

"I will try when it's finished. I haven't had too much time lately."

"Is this done in charcoal?"

"Yes, an Indian girl I knew."

"I like it."

"Is this nude on a bed in the moonlight in ultraviolet paint?"

"Yes."

"How does that paint work?"

"I'll show you." I pulled out the small black light lamp, and turning it on, held it up to the painting. "Wow, it looks like moonlight on her. The sky through the window looks a million miles away. I have never seen anything like it. It is beautiful. Can't you sell things like that?"

"I think so. I haven't tried yet."

"I like all your paintings. I like the nude best. They look so real. How do you do it?" You embraced me in what seemed to be utter admiration.

"Hard work and plenty of practice."

"And you never studied painting in school?"

"No. I never had time. I was always doing something else." I could hear a car in the driveway. My folks must be returning.

They came in and did not act upset or greatly disturbed.

"Hi. Mom, Pop. Did we give you a scare?"

"A little," Mom said.

"We weren't too worried. You are old enough to take care of yourself. We did think maybe the car broke down and you could not get help. So, we went looking," Pop explained.

"We did get stuck in the sand at the ocean, but we got a tow truck this morning and here we are ready for lunch."

"Well, I've got to get back to work." Pop headed for the door.

"I'm sorry we worried you."

"I'm used to your crazy stunts by now. That is what makes life around here interesting," he said, trying to be dismissive of the potential seriousness that did not transpire.

Mother and you and I talked for quite a while after Pop left. Mother was clearly trying to make you feel comfortable. She rambled on about the raising of her family through the tough days of the Great Depression. How we managed and stayed together through it all. When we moved here, we lived in a surplus army squad tent for two years before building this shack but we are going to build a real house next year. Pop was a jack of all trades and we could do it all ourselves. You listened with interest.

"Why don't you come and stay with us for a while?" mom said.

"I'd like to, but I don't want to hurt my parents."

"You do what you think best, You're welcome anytime."

"If I remember correctly, I'm supposed to haul some trash to the dump today. So, if you will excuse me, I'll be going," I said.

I felt at ease leaving you there with Mom. She liked you and you would like her. I would not worry about you for a while. I was back in half an hour. The two of you were still chatting when I returned. It was good to come in and see you two so relaxed and obviously enjoying each other. I sat down and we continued talking about nothing. You were in good spirits. We used up the day that way until mother noticed it was 5:00 o'clock in the evening.

"I think I'd better go now," you said. "I have to bathe and set my hair."

In the car you threw your arms around my neck and said you loved me and my folks. It was hard to leave you at your door. You bounced from the car to the door of your house, happier than I had ever seen you. When I backed down the driveway and looked back at the door you were there waving goodbye. I blinked the car lights to let you know I had seen you. I suddenly remembered I was to see the doctor at nine o'clock. When I got home, I fed the ducks and chickens before Pop got home. I mulled the day's events as I did the chores. We had dinner at 8:00 o'clock and I got ready to go see the doctor.

CHAPTER 22

YOUR DOCTOR

It was dark when I arrived at the doctor's office. The streetlamps added to my mood. I usually felt small beside streetlamps, but tonight they were just utilities to light my way. I walked into the building, down the hall and into the receiving room. I saw no one there. I heard a voice saying he would be out in a minute. I looked at the clock. I was exactly on time.

"Come into my office," the doctor said around the door. "Cigarette?" he offered, as I entered the room. He showed me a chair as he motioned for me to sit down, as he did the same.

"Well, how is everything?" he began.

"She seemed to be in good spirits when I took her home."

"Whatever happened to you two last night?"

"She wanted to get drunk..." I told him the whole story, getting stuck in the sand, and not getting home until late morning.

"What are your intentions toward her?"

"Well, if it all works out, I want to marry her."

"Are you sure it's not just a case of you having your ego bolstered by the fact that she's obviously looking up to you as her savior. It would be quite easy for you to mistake ego satisfaction for love. I can tell you that women often fall in love with their doctors. I know. So, you see, she may think she is in love with you because you have been good to her. And you in turn may think you're in love with her because she makes you feel important and respected."

"I don't know the answer to any of that. I know she says she wants material security; things money can give her. I cannot offer that now."

"Do you think you can do that in the future?"

"No, I can't give her a lot of money." He smiled as if he thought he had shown me something.

"But I don't think money is what really makes people happy. I think love is what people want....to love and be loved, to need and be needed. I guess I believe that love is really what she wants and needs and in time will realize it. I think in all of her love relationships she has felt used, and so she doesn't trust it."

"And you think you can show her she can be loved without feeling used?"

"That's the way I feel."

"That's a pretty ambitious program. Do you really think you can do it?"

"I don't know, but I have to try. Who else is there to help her? I cannot walk away and let her fight this battle alone when she trusts me to help. Besides, I have always loved her."

We talked for almost two hours. He said your mother might call in a psychiatrist. I asked him if he thought you needed one. He said he could not say. He did think you should get out of that house and away from your mother and sister for a while. I looked at my watch and realized I had to get some sleep. "It's late. I'd better go," I said and thanked him for his interest.

"Feel free to stop by anytime and bring her with you if you like," he said. I went home and had the best sleep I had had for days.

CHAPTER 23

DANCING

It was Wednesday. I did not wake until nearly noon. I called your house to see if you had gone to school. You were still sleeping. I said I would be over and not to wake you. When I arrived, I was informed that your mother had made an appointment for you with a psychiatrist at two o'clock. Your father asked if I would take you since your mother had taken their car. Also, he did not think you would go with anyone else. I was not entirely pleased about the psychiatrist, but that was not my decision to make. They apparently had not told you about the appointment. You appeared in your bathrobe. I had to get you to the appointment by two o'clock. I decided a bit of subterfuge was in order. We could have a confrontation later by ourselves. Too many people complicate things around here.

"Would you like to go shopping with me?" I asked deceitfully.

"Alright," you said happily.

"Better hurry up, I have to get to town by two." We were halfway to town before I told you that I was really taking you to an appointment with a psychiatrist that your mother had arranged. You did not want to go. I said I was not happy about it either, but your folks needed to feel like they were doing something to help that would give them some sense of comfort. They felt a responsibility, and this was their effort to face it. The best thing you could do was to be as calm and cooperative as you could to convince the psychiatrist you did not need any therapy. That you really owed them that much. You finally agreed. You did well. The psychiatrist simply advised you to come back next week if you felt the need. We went downtown to do the shopping I had promised. Later I took you to my house and we relaxed until mother woke up— she had to work tonight, and I did not want to disturb her sleep. Pop came in and I figured it was time to take you home. You said you had to dance tonight, and I needed some sleep. After dinner I laid down to rest. The phone rang. "Hi," I said, I knew it was you.

"Tonight is your last night off this week isn't?" you said.

"Yes."

"You said you wanted to see us dance. Well, why don't you go with us tonight?"

"That's a great idea. Does it cost anything to just watch?"

"No, but I'll give you money for a drink at the bar if you like."

"When do you want to leave?"

"Half an hour."

"I'll be there."

Your sister drove, and we sat in the back seat enjoying the ride. It was dark and the sky clear and filled with stars. At the hotel we had time for coffee before the first show. After the coffee we went to the Hawaiian Room. There was an elaborate set up featuring a large space in the middle of the room which was an actual body of water called the lagoon. Floating on this pond was a barge with a smooth deck covered over by a huge umbrella-like awning. You had to go change for the show. As you left you put your hand in my pocket. I did not pay much attention to that until I sat at the bar and poked my hand in my pocket to find a wadded up five-dollar bill. I did not need it because Pop had given me five dollars when I left home. I put the bill in my wallet and ordered a Rum Collins. About then it rained on the lagoon. A startling effect, but quite pleasant. I sipped my drink, lit a cigarette, and looked around at the people at the bar and those at the tables surrounding the lagoon. The barge was tied up at the edge of the lagoon. You and your sister appeared and stepped aboard the barge and began to dance to the music of a small band playing Hawaiian music. The barge, attached to ropes, was pulled to the middle of the lagoon and the show was on. Colored spotlights danced on you and your sister while the rain came in soft intermittent showers. It was lovely and you did not even get wet. I watched you move gracefully around the deck of the barge. Your hands made such smooth, flowing gestures, they did not seem to have bones in them. You were to me, utter fascination. I had never seen you dance, and it was thrilling and exotic to witness. The show ended and you left the barge. After a short interval we met and went across the street to a neighboring hotel. In the bar on the top floor of that hotel we sat and looked out the huge windows at the night sky and the lamp-lit streets below. I wondered if those little dots walking around down there had any idea we were looking at them. Eventually I turned my gaze from the night scene out of the window and found myself looking straight into your beautiful eyes. I squeezed your hand and said,

"I love you."

"Me too," you replied.

"What time is it?" your sister asked.

"Quarter to twelve," I said

"We have to do the last show in fifteen minutes," she said.

I enjoyed the last show as much as the first.

After the show we went for a snack in China Town and then home. At your door I said, "Why don't you come home with me tonight?" You said you wanted to but could not. I drove home wishing you could.

CHAPTER 24

"SHE CALLED CHICAGO"

The next day I worried about you. I seemed to always worry about you unless you were with me. I did not see you until I brought you over for dinner. You could not stay long, and I had to take you home so you could get ready for work. We sat in your driveway and talked a bit. I gave in to the impulse and said, "Will you marry me?" You did not answer. I was not surprised. I figured you were going to say no, but the silence was hard to deal with. I wished I had not said it.

"I do and I don't," you finally spoke.

"I know, you don't want to be tied down. Right?" I tried to disguise my disappointment by sounding mature.

"I want to travel. I don't know why, but I just like to travel."

"It's getting late. We can talk about this later. I know you have to get ready for work and so do I." I went home, feeling twisted, got ready, and went to work.

The next day was Friday. I picked you up at three o'clock. We had dinner at my house, and we revisited the subject of marriage. It began by you saying, "Let's get married." I was somewhat shocked by the abruptness but giddy at the proposal.

"You're on." I was not at all sure you would not change your mind, but I was open to wishful thinking. I asked you to stay the night, but you could not because you had things to do early in the morning.

"I won't be able to see you tomorrow." You explained that you had to go shopping and do laundry and would be too busy. I was so happy I did not press the issue. I took you home and was at work within an hour.

The next evening, I phoned you about six. You were in a good mood. At eight-fifteen your mother phoned me. "Did she tell you she called Chicago last night?"

"No. What about?"

"She called Chicago last night when she thought we were all asleep. She told him to send her the money."

That was all she knew. She had no more details but thought I should know this much. It made no sense. How could she want to get married and then the same day phone Chicago to send money? There must be a reasonable explanation, but I could not think of one at the moment. I went to work at 10:00 PM, got home at 7:30 AM, and did not know what to do. I had planned to pick you up at three or four in the afternoon, but I simply had to see you now.

"Wake up sleepy head," I said looking down at you in your bed. You finally peeped from under slow lids and smiled.

"Aren't you a little early?"

"Yes, but I wanted to see you before I went to bed."

"Well, if you go out, I'll get dressed."

I went to pour coffee. Over coffee I did not mention the phone call. I wanted you to bring it up. We left for my house. You still said nothing about it. At my house I asked you about the phone call to Chicago. You were shocked that anyone knew about it. You thought they were all asleep. I pushed it further. You still refused to talk about it. I insisted. Finally, you said you did not know why you did it. That did not work for me as a good enough or even believable answer.

"Don't lie to me. I don't lie to you, so don't lie to me."

"Would you believe me if I said I didn't love you?"

"No. If you can't tell me the truth, don't say anything."

"OK. I did it because I don't want to hurt you."

"That makes no sense. It is not that you called that hurts, it's that you did not tell me. I might be able to accept that you must leave, but not to tell me at all and then just leave. That really hurts. What you are really saying is you want to hurt me because you don't want to hurt me."

"I'm sorry," you sounded a little contrite.

"Are you leaving then?"

"What else can I do? If I stay, I will get tired of being in one place and go anyway. I love you and don't want to do that to you."

"Let me get this straight. You have decided you do not want to marry me. Is that right?"

"Not exactly, I do want to marry you, but I don't want to hurt you, and if we get married, I would end up hurting you because I would get tired and restless and have to go. That is how I am. I'm sorry, but it's true," you said it fatalistically.

"Then you intend to go to the guy in Chicago?" I said with resignation.

"What else can I do? I want to sing and travel. If I marry you, I can't do either one."

"I suppose that's means you'll marry him," it was as much a question as a statement.

"No, I don't love him."

"What if he won't let you sing if you don't."

"I'll talk him out of it."

Imagining you with him was too painful for me to dwell on what might or might not be. I was out of arguments.

There was nothing left for me to do. You were going away, out of my life. How could there be happiness ever again?

"I can't let you go." I should not have spoken. Hearing the words multiplied the rejection to such a level of self-pity I could not stop the tears I felt rolling down my cheeks. I was ashamed and powerless to control myself. I buried my head in the pillow and sobbed. After a time, I felt myself relaxing. I was tired, all done in. I never liked the notion of a man crying, but now I had to accept it. At last, I lifted my face, and ashamed but helpless as a child, tried to say, "You can't just go away," but my chin quivered uncontrollably, and the words came out childlike and stupid.

"I'm sorry, I'm sorry," you said holding me close and caressing me like a mother consoling a wounded child.

"I thought I could do it, but I guess I can't," I stammered.

"Do what?"

"Show you love is more important than anything else. I cannot do it. I don't know how."

"It's not your fault. I'm just no good," you said with some emotion.

"Do you want some coffee?" You searched for something to regain a semblance of normal behavior.

"I don't want anything," I heard the sarcasm in my voice and was instantly sorry for it.

"I'm sorry," I apologized. "I guess coffee would taste good right now."

Witnessing my collapse had a decided effect on you. You treated me with more care. I wondered if you had needed to see me more vulnerable than I had ever wished or allowed myself to be.

I heard a slight noise and Mother emerged from the other room.

"I thought you two would be in Reno getting married by now," she said. She was obviously curious.

"I have to work tonight," I said. Your eyes pleaded with me not tell everything we had been through.

"Can I stay here tonight?" you asked.

"Yes, of course," Mother said.

I drove to work that night thinking about all that had transpired in this crazy day. It seemed clear that you were going to leave, but your asking to stay overnight gave me a thread of comfort that I would see you in the morning. That was enough to get through the night.

CHAPTER 25

DON'T MENTION IT

When I got home in the morning, I found you asleep. I leaned over you and kissed your forehead. You moved a little.

"Good morning, Princess," I said.

"Hi," you said, wetting your lips and squinting your eyes against the morning.

"Sleep good?"

"Uh huh."

"Want some coffee?"

"Mm."

I brought the coffee and sat on the edge of the bed, carefully placing my cup on the night table next to yours. I looked at your morning face and swore I saw love in there for me. You sat up, threw your arms around me, and we kissed, and my heart cried for joy. What a life that would be to come home to.

"You are all through dancing, aren't you?" I said.

"Yes, night before last. You must be tired."

"I am."

"Well, if you'll make yourself scarce, I'll get dressed and you can go to bed. I have it all warmed up for you." We had some breakfast, and I went to bed.

"Are you staying all day?" I asked.

"What time do you want me to wake you?"

"I usually get up around three." I went to sleep and must have dreamed but could not recall.

You had hot coffee ready when three o'clock. came around. You were chatty and charming.

"Tell me what you did at work last night."

"Oh, I worked on the CD Ward."

"What's CD?"

"It means: Contagious Disease. It's the ward where they keep highly contagious disease cases until they're cleared-up."

"You have never talked about your job. Tell me more about the hospital."

"Well, the hospital is for people who were born with deficiencies of the brain and body."

"You mean a mental institution?"

"No, not exactly. The kind of mental institution you are thinking of is for patients who have normal capacities but have gotten mixed up in the way they think. Our patients, on the other hand, do not have normal brain and body development. Some are like children and will never develop beyond that level. There are many different forms of handicaps. We have them all."

"It sounds interesting. I would like to go there and see them some time."

"Maybe you would even like to work there."

"Maybe I would like that. Can you take me there to visit?"

You seemed to be reorganizing your plans. What a great idea, both of us working at the hospital. I began to weave new dreams.

"What do you have to do to get a job there?"

"You have to take a State Examination. They give the tests on the second Wednesday of each month. The next one will be...Tomorrow! There will be an exam tomorrow morning at ten o'clock. Do you want to try?

"Yes, I would like to try. Do you think I can do it?"

"I will try to prepare you. I have things you can read."

I handed you some books and went to bed. I was exhausted. I slept until four o'clock in the afternoon.

"Are you awake?" You asked standing over ne.

"I think I'm getting there."

"Did you sleep well?"

"I died. I was all in. Got some coffee?"

"Right away."

I watched you walk to the other end of the room where the kitchen was. You poured the coffee and returned. I saw mother sitting at the table doing something, I could not tell what. You set the coffee down and sat beside me, lit a cigarette, and handed it to me. This was the life.

"I love you," you said in the sweetest way.

"I love you too," I said. "What have you been doing all day?"

"I read the material you gave me, then your mother and I went to do some shopping. We did the laundry and now we aren't doing anything."

"Have you learned anything?"

"Just ask me a question."

"OK. What's the largest bone in the body?"

"The femur," you said without hesitating. I was impressed.

"Name the shoulder bone."

"The scapula".

"What is the patella?"

"The knee cap."

"The humerus?"

"The upper arm bone."

"Tibia?"

"The lower part of the leg between the knee and the ankle."

"Sternum?"

"Breastbone."

"OK. For the bones. What is peritonitis?"

"It's an inflammation. An inflammation of...the...I can't remember."

"Well, that's fairly good. It is an inflammation of the peritoneum. The space under the diaphragm, below the ribs." I was pleased. You had certainly applied yourself. I got dressed and went out to feed the ducks and chickens. When I came back, you were helping mother with dinner. I was elated at your participation in these simple domestic chores and how you seemed to be genuinely enjoying them. You said you hated housework, but here you were doing it with enthusiasm.

After dinner we sat and watched television until nine-thirty when I had to leave for work.

I kissed you and left. The shift was uneventful.

CHAPTER 26

THE TEST

On the way home I planned the day's activities. We would leave home in time to take the test at ten o'clock. It would take fifteen minutes to fill out the forms and half an hour to drive to the hospital. If we left between eight forty-five and nine o'clock, we should have no trouble.

You were still asleep when I got home at seven-thirty. You got dressed and appeared from my folks' bedroom wearing a black wool skirt with charcoal threads running through it, making the skirt look charcoal rather than black. The skirt accentuated the curve of your hips perfectly. Your blouse was black cotton with a one-inch trim of gold around the moderately low neckline. Over the blouse you wore a white short-sleeved half sweater that only buttoned at the top. You were a picture. You certainly knew how to dress. Your dark hair and lashes completed the image of casually exotic beauty. We left the house at nine exactly and reached the hospital at nine-thirty, filled out the application form and discovered the exam was rescheduled for eleven. We toured the grounds, and I pointed out all the different cottages, each specializing in a particular type of patient according to age and diagnosis. The facility was huge with more than fifteen cottages, a large hospital and a large cafeteria for ambulatory patients and staff. There was a laundry, and a large farm which raised meat and vegetables for institutional consumption. The ambulatory patients who could perform menial labor tasks were utilized wherever possible in maintaining the farm, laundry, and grounds. All in all it was a smooth functioning establishment. Some of the cottages housed severely damaged individuals, including microcephalus and hydrocephalus cases along with babies exhibiting a host of not-so-common birth defects. We finished the tour, driving slowly through the well-manicured grounds which looked for all the world like a prosperous college campus.

While you took the test, I went to the cafeteria and drank coffee.

You emerged from the test smiling but looking a bit tired.

"How was it?" asked.

"I don't think I passed."

"Don't be too sure. I did not think I passed either. If you didn't you can still try again next time." I tried to counter your doubts. "You'll get the results in about two weeks."

"I hope I passed," you said sincerely.

"Can I interest you in some food?"

"I can always eat."

We walked to the cafeteria and chatted over lunch. I drove home over the mountain to enjoy the scenic view, but much had happened since that first ride. Today it was overcast, and the splendor of fall was nowhere to be seen.

CHAPTER 27

PLAYING HOUSE

Thursday morning, I got home by seven-thirty. The day was uneventful. I needed to catch up with my sleep. I would be off for the next two days, so I slept until three.

You were attentive when I woke up. We had coffee over a midday breakfast. We chatted about insignificant things like whether to go see a movie or not. There was nothing playing that we both wanted to see. Mother and Pop did go out for the evening and we were alone.

"Let's just stay home," you finally said and meant it. After dinner I decided to pose you for a painting. I placed you on the divan in a long loose summer dress. You laid there looking serene and beautiful. I moved the lamp around for the best light and started to work. I was lost in another world for two hours. It was the first time I had been able to work directly from looking at you. The likeness was good, and I was happy. As I cleaned my brushes you asked, "What are you going to do tomorrow?"

"I thought I would take you to the city for your doctor's visit. Then we can go to China Town after that and do some Christmas shopping. There's only two weeks left."

"When should we leave?" you asked.

"About two, I think."

We arrived in the city at three o'clock. It was raining. There was something romantic about a rainy day in the city. First, we went to see your doctor, a Chinese herbalist. He prescribed Herbal concoctions for most common ailments according to ancient compounding formulas. You got something for headaches and skin cleansing. I was entitled to a free checkup and I decided it could not hurt.

After checking me over he said, "Young man, I don't see why you should have such high blood pressure. How old are you?"

"Twenty-two."

"Your blood pressure should be 120 over 80, but its 170 over 90. Do you have dizzy spells?"

"No."

"Do you perspire easily?"

"Not too."

"Do you drink?"

"Alcohol? Not very often".

"How often?"

"Maybe three times a month."

"What else do you drink?"

"Coffee."

"How much?"

"Maybe ten cups a day I'm not sure exactly."

"You had better cut down. You better take care of it now before it gets worse."

"How many should I drink?"

"Three should be enough."

I thanked him kindly for his advice and wondered if I would think to take his advice. We browsed through the stores in China Town looking for Christmas presents. We wandered the rainy streets, soaking up the sense of antiquity that was everywhere. It began to get dark and the lights came on. We rummaged through curious little shops and bought exotic Chinese candies that you picked out for me: spicy plums that puckered my lips and were hot, sweet, and sour all at the same time. Everything in China Town was a mass of leaning lines. Nothing looked straight, plumb, or square, just rickety, and old, yet permanent and eternal as time itself. What a wonderful world to be in with you

"How about something to eat." I said.

"What do you want to eat?"

"Let's go to the Green Dragon Palace over there." I pointed across the street to the painted sign of a huge green dragon with gold teeth.

We went in loaded down with packages of all sizes. The dining area was elevated above the main floor which featured a dim lit bar. We went past the bar and up several steps to the dining cubicles, with their green privacy curtains. We unloaded our packages on the extra chairs and sat down. A waiter appeared and explained that there were no menus at this time. I never could figure out what was the reason, but it did not matter. You chattered with him and we sat and waited for the food. You explained to me that you had ordered soup, BBQ spareribs, shrimp cooked in bacon and tomato sauce, fried rice, and Chinese vegetables. There was plenty of tea. I looked at you across the candlelit table and wondered if this could possibly last. How I loved you. "Have you had fun today?" I asked.

"I can't remember when I had so much fun."

"Even though we spent all of our money?"

"I'm glad we spent it all."

"So am I. This is one of the nicest days I can remember."

Dinner came and we ate. The chopsticks were fun to learn for me; you were a pro. I accidentally brushed a chopstick on the floor with my sleeve and the waiter appeared from behind the curtain reprimanding me. Saying I should always place them toward the center of the table. He then gave me a new pair and removed the old ones. I smiled in apology and embarrassment. I made sure that did not happen again. You were kind enough not seem to notice my blunder.

I paid the check and made it back to the car with our packages.

"What did you do with our fortunes from the cookies?" you asked.

"I put them all in my pocket." We managed to get two each. "You want to read them again?"

"Yes."

"Read aloud," I said fishing them out of my shirt pocket and handing them to you.   "I'm going to have a big family.... that is one of mine," you said. "You are going to do something that will bring great credit upon yourself. That is yours. People are going to like me that I thought did not...that's mine and the last is yours. You must be patient a while longer."

"A lot to think about," I said starting the engine. It rained all the way home, but it was a warm pleasant rain.

CHAPTER 28

"I CAN'T STAY"

The next day was Saturday and it rained all day. Mother and father and you and I just loafed all day. The day passed pleasantly. I had to work tonight so I planned to take a nap around five o'clock PM. Earlier you said you wanted to go to your house for a while to take some presents over. I gave you the car keys and reminded you dinner would be at five. You returned at five, we ate, and then I went off for a nap. I got up at nine-thirty and left at ten.

"I'll see you in the morning around seven-thirty," I said going out the door.

When I got home you were sound asleep. I kissed you gently and you woke up, stretching your arms up and around my neck, and whispering in my ear, "I love you."

"Me too," I said, instantly realizing my implausible English, but not thinking it worthy of much dwelling upon. It was Sunday. No one was up. Everyone saw the rain as a good excuse to sleep in. I spread my sleeping bag on top of the bed next to you and climbed in. I was tired and we exchanged just a few words before I was sound asleep.

I woke at five PM. and you were gone. Mother said you had gone home for a while. I was supposed to pick you up at five. I dressed and left for your house. The rain came in torrents. When I returned with you, we had dinner and sat around watching television. I tried to think of something to do. I remembered the qipao dress I had bought you in China Town. It was jade green with lovely embroidery and a small slit at the hem line. The collar needed to be lowered slightly and some tucks sewn around the waist. I knew how to do these things because I had always been a curious child and Mother a ready teacher of domestic chores. I removed the collar with a razor blade, then repositioned and marked the center with a piece of hand soap. I finished sewing the collar in time to go to work. Before I left, I began to get the feeling that something was bothering you. There was not time for a lengthy conversation. It ended up with a simple statement from you. "I think I'll go home for a few days."

"You're feeling restless, aren't you?" I said, knowing I was right.

"You always seem to know."

"Just promise you won't go away or do anything without talking to me."

"OK."

I left for work with a premonition that tomorrow was going to be unsettling. One part of me wanted to believe that your love for me would not let you leave; the other part was not so sure. In the end I would just have to see what the morning brought.

It was still raining when I got home the next morning. I parked the car and went into the house. You were still sleeping. You were customarily affectionate when I woke you.

"You still want to go home today?"

"Yes," you answered slowly.

"Well, I wonder how long you plan to be away?"

"Would it hurt you terribly if I said I didn't want to stay here anymore?" You spoke hesitantly but deliberately. I did not answer. There was no answer to that question. You knew before you asked how I would feel. You only made it a question to soften the impact. Nevertheless, the impact could not be softened. I looked past you at the wall as if the answer might be written there. It was not. I kept staring, wordless.

"I tried not to let this happen," you said, "but I just got restless. There is nothing that can be done about it. I'm sorry."

"If you get restless staying with us, won't you get restless staying at your folks' house too? Where will you go from there? Chicago?"

"I suppose so."

"Don't want to wait and see if you passed the exam?"

"I know I didn't," you sounded sure.

"But what if you did?"

"It wouldn't matter, I'd get tired of that even if I went to work there. Then I'd have to leave."

"Everyone gets tired of things from time to time, but they learn to get through it. You're not even trying to work it out."

"I know all that. I don't want to talk about it."

"I guess we're just not suited to each other after all," I said, not totally meaning it.

"What do you mean?"

"I would like to marry you, but I couldn't just pick up and go every time you got restless. I have obligations that require me to stay in one place. For example, right now, I could not leave until next June when my car will be paid for. And even then, I would have to have a job to go to. I just cannot quit work without knowing I have another job where I am going. My life must have some order to it and a plan for the future. At least enough of a plan to know I will be able to support myself, buy food and have a place to sleep. Growing up in the depression left its mark on me. I must have a job. I have seen how people must live when they do not have work. I do not want to ever be in that position. I have this job at the hospital, and I can't give it up without a better job to go to."

"I guess I better get ready and go home," you said.

You put on your gown and went to the other room to change. You emerged looking gorgeous. I wanted to kiss you. I did and it was good.

"I love you," I said.

"Do you really?"

"Yes, from the first time I ever saw you, and I will forever. I can't help myself."

I took you home and wondered on the way home how long we had together before you left. I was beginning to accept the inevitability of losing you, but I secretly hoped that your love for me might overcome this need you had to run from your demons, or whatever it was that you were trying to get away from. I went to bed. At five o'clock I got up, did the chores, and had dinner before phoning you. "Hi, Princess, what have you been doing all day?"

"Oh, I baked bread and did the dishes, everyone was shocked over here. They didn't think I could do it."

"That's great. How do you feel?"

"I feel very good. I have been really busy all day."

"I'm glad."

"When are you coming over for abalone dinner?" you asked.

"When are you serving it?"

"Whenever you want to eat it."

"How about tomorrow?"

"Fine. We eat at five. You'll be here then?"

"With bells on."

"I missed you today," you said in a lower voice and clearly meaning it.

"I missed you too," I said.

"We'll see you tomorrow at five then. Right?"

"Right," I felt good again.

CHAPTER 29

A LAST SUPPER

The dinner was excellent. I ate generously of everything. Abalone properly prepared is a great delicacy. After the meal everyone left the table to watch television. I turned to you and said I needed to get gas in the car.

"Would you like to join me?" You put on a sweater and we left. After filling the gas-tank, I asked what you would like to do.

"I don't care."

I drove to the secluded spot where we had parked one night in the rain. I remembered it was three weeks since we had parked there. It was a murky night. The rain had been steady for a week, but it was not raining just now, but could start anytime. The sky was overcast, and the air was wet. The ground was wet. Everything was wet.

"Don't get stuck," you said.

"I couldn't get stuck here if I wanted to. This used to be a shale pit. The ground is solid shale for several feet straight down."

"That's good," you said.
I reclined the seats and we lay there, side by side. I broke the silence. "What have you decided to do?"

"I'm going to leave. I know that much."

"Chicago?"

"No, I waited too long. I do not think he has a job for me anymore. No, not Chicago, but I am going somewhere. I don't know where yet, but somewhere."

"You just get tired of everything and have to go."

"Yes."

"Have you gotten tired of me too?"

"No, but down deep I'm afraid I might."

There was nothing left for me to say or do. I took you home and tried again to reconcile my impending heartache.

All the way home from work the next morning I felt I had to talk to you. I decided to go to see you as soon as you were up. I waited until nine o'clock before I phoned. You had just gotten up. I said I would be over and to put the coffee on.

You looked sleepy when I arrived.

"Hi," you yawned.

"Good morning," I said wide awake.

We went into your bedroom, shut the door, and sat on the edge of your unmade bed.

"What's on your mind?" you asked.

"About what?"

"Us......Well?"

"Have you changed your mind about leaving yet?"

"No, only...well. You won't like this".

"What won't I like?"

"I called Chicago last night after you left."

"And?"

"The job is still waiting."

"So, you'll be leaving for Chicago soon?"

"I don't know how soon, but yes."

"It's your life. Go ahead."

"You aren't angry?"

"Damn it, of course I'm angry. I do not want you to go, and I think it is a mistake, but if you have to go...then go. I can't stop you."

"I love you," you said, throwing your arms around me. I could tell that you meant it, but you also meant it when you said you were leaving. I began to realize you could mean both things at the same time. "Do you still love me?" you said interrupting my thoughts.

"Yes, with all my heart and soul."

"I'm glad you love me."

"I don't know why. It isn't going to do either of us any good when you leave."

"Why not?"

"Well, you're going to be too busy to think of me" I was saying.

"I won't be able to keep from thinking about you," you interrupted. "You are the only one I ever loved. I tried many times to love, but you are the only one. I didn't believe there was such a thing until I fell in love with you."

"This is the silliest thing I ever heard. You cannot stay and I can't go, yet we are both madly in love. Does that make any sense?"

"No, but it's the truth."

I held you and you put your head on my shoulder, and I could feel you breathing against me. Oh, the sweet and sour of it!

"Promise me that if you ever feel depressed or down, you will call me. I will always be here."

"Yes," you whispered through a tear. There was no sob, just one little tear in the corner of your eye. You seemed so helpless I wanted to cry just looking at you. Your eyes were scanning my face. They were wide and big and beautiful and searching. All I could see was a scared, hurt, and lonely little girl. How could I let you go? What in the hell was I supposed to do? I looked at my watch. It was noon. I had to go home and get some sleep. I still had to go to work tonight.

"I've got to go home," I said softly.

"Don't go. You can sleep here."

"No, Mother expects me home to do some things for her. I do have to go."

"Alright." You held on to me all the way to the door and did not want to let go even then. As I drove home thinking over all that had been said, it seemed all the words were about your leaving and all the feelings were about how much we love each other. What next?

CHAPTER 30

NEW YEARS EVE

In the days that followed we avoided talk of marriage or Chicago. I did not mind. I just wanted to enjoy you as long as I could, one day at a time. We had fun and were happy those days. Christmas came and went. The holidays passed uneventfully.

New Year's Eve came, and we decided to have a party. You and I and a friend of mine with your sister. We were all at my friend's house. His parents were gone for the weekend. We had three bottles of vodka and plenty of mixer. The radio played soft music and the lights were low, so we danced.

"I'm not much of a dancer," I whispered in your ear.

"You're doing alright," you whispered back.

"Would you care for another drink?" I asked.

"Uh huh."

I poured two drinks and we sat ignoring your sister and my friend. They were having a good time. I looked at my watch. It was five minutes to midnight.

"Another year about to go," you said.

"I hope the next one is better," I said.

"This one hasn't been so bad," you said. "We fell in love, didn't we?"

The roar and din of all the various contrivances of man became apparent as the clock struck midnight. The noises came from outside and all the corners of the world. There were shotgun blasts and cars roaring and backfiring, horns blowing and noises defying description.

"Hey, it's New Years!" your sister and my friend shouted at us.

"Is that what it is? I thought that we were invaded," I shouted back. I turned to you and asked if you were still going to Chicago. You said, "Next week."

"Flying?"

"No, I'm taking the train."

"Mind if I drive you to the train?

"You don't have to."

"I know, but I want to."

"OK. If you want to."

CHAPTER 31

TO THE TRAIN

Later, the rain had stopped, and the sun glistened on the wet road as I approached the toll gate to the bridge.

"Hey, wake up. Here's the money for the bridge toll." You handed me the money for the toll. I had been just staring at the road ahead preoccupied with memories of you and the events of the last few months. I paid the toll and drove on into the city and parked in front of the train depot at three twenty in the afternoon. You only had to wait for ten minutes. I carried your bags to the freight department and brought you the baggage checks. I looked full at you as I handed you the checks. I had avoided doing that until now, but I realized this might be the last time I ever saw you and I must have the memory. You were beautiful.

"You don't mind if I walk you to the platform, do you?" I asked a little choked.

"Of course, I don't mind."

I have never seen so many people. Some coming, some going, all shouting to be heard. Young folks, old folks and kids getting in the way of everything and being pulled this way and that. The noise of a train pulling in on another track was adding an additional level to the chaos. If all these people get to where they are going, and no one gets lost I will have to bow to the utter miracle of it. We finally reached the boarding platform.

"Do you have your tickets?" I asked. You showed them to me in silent reply.

"All aboard!" shouted a man with a ticket punch in his un-gloved hand.

"I guess this is goodbye," I said slowly.

"I guess so."

"May I kiss you goodbye?"

"I was going to ask if you would."

I kissed you and remembered all the sweet things we had shared.

"I love you. I will not forget you," you said into my ear with more emotion than you had intended.

"I love you too," I said choking on the words.

"Will you write to me?"

"Of course. You must write first so I know the address. OK?"

"OK."

"All aboard!"

There was a tear in your eye as you handed the man the ticket. I watched you disappear through the doorway as the train seemed to swallow you up. I tried to find you in a window, but you were out of sight. I turned and walked slowly down the platform. The platform was still wet, and the sun glistening off the concrete was so blinding it made my eyes water.

CHAPTER 32

AFTERWARD

When you disappeared into the train that day it was the last time I ever saw you. Your sister invited me to lunch a year later and showed me a photo of you and your little daughter. You had married the guy in Chicago. You did not become a singer.

Your sister and I talked long about your moods and fears and only then did I learn that your mother was Japanese and that the three of you had been interred in a concentration camp on the west coast during the war. I also learned that your mother was a very resourceful woman who managed somehow to get special privileges from the Governor for favors not mentioned and that you had been molested as a little girl by one of the guards. This was a bombshell to me. It could explain all the bad dreams and unreasoning fears. How I wished you had been able to tell me. The thought of it brings tears to my eyes to this day. Why had no one mentioned this to me before?

Your sister went on to explain how your mother had wanted to be a dancer and came up with the idea of teaching her girls to be hula dancers and tour as Hawaiian Sisters. Was it to give you a new identity? Better to be Hawaiian than Japanese? I began to understand why you hated dancing. I felt that these revelations solved the riddle of your bad dreams. What about mine? We had the same dream. Your bad dream was the result of childhood trauma which you were apparently unwilling or unable to acknowledge. I had no such trauma...or did I?

How strange the things our minds do to ignore unpleasant events of the past. I have learned to put out of my conscious mind, most of the time, the fact that I was the victim of a childhood accident in which my legs suffered third degree burns and I was in and out of hospitals for five years before multiple skin grafts made it possible for me to walk again. I could never go swimming or wear shorts like other people. I had to hide those scars from everyone forever. Around girls I was always afraid of exposure. Indeed, you and I were both deeply wounded as children. I carefully hid it from others. In high school I always had a doctor's excuse for not taking gym. I effectively hid it from my consciousness behind a carefully memorized, impenetrable wall, which simply said to my conscious mind "never take you pants off." I developed a kind of amnesia from this denial. Yes, I could understand why you could not talk about your wound, I could not talk about mine either.

Life went on. Pop secured a loan at the lumber yard, and I learned carpentry. He and I built what turned out to be the best-looking house on the street. He was a perfectionist on a mission. I paid off my car and applied myself with greater concentration to my college studies.

One day your sister phoned me to inform me you had overdosed on heroine. You were gone. I would never see you again. You were the most beautiful girl I had ever known, and you were no more. Dear God, how I loved you. There is a tear in my heart that will never go away. Eventually I met a beautiful young woman who accepted me for myself. We married and had three lovely children. She too is beautiful, and I have painted many pictures of her. She does not know, nor does anyone else, how often you come to me at night in the sacred privacy of my dreams. Sleep in peace, Dear Princess. I love you still.

THE END